GHOSTS AMONG THE GUMTREES

AMRA PAJALIĆ

MELBOURNE, AUSTRALIA

https://www.pishukinpress.com/

First Published 2026 by Pishukin Press

Cover design: Created using Canva elements, cover image attribution Photo byClicksbySaggu via Depositphotos

Editing Support: I use ProWritingAid and Sudowrite, both of which incorporate artificial intelligence, to support the editing and revision process. I'm committed to transparency and quality, and AI is used as a creative aid while I retain full control over all artistic and editorial decisions.

For content and trigger warnings please go towww.amrapajalic.com/themes

Quality control: We care about producing error-free books. If you discover a typo or formatting issue, please contact admin@pishukinpress.com

Paperback Edition: 9781922871596

Content Warnings

www.amrapajalic.com/themes.html

Glossary

Ćevapi, skinless beef sausages

Fildžan-demitasse coffee cup

Džezva-coffee pot

Minaret-a slender tower, typically part of a mosque, with a balcony from which a muezzin calls Muslims to prayer.

Hadiths-a collection of traditions containing sayings of the prophet Muhammad which, with accounts of his daily practice (the Sunna), constitute the major source of guidance for Muslims apart from the Quran.

Mihrab-a niche indicating the direction of Mecca that all Muslims prayed too.

Potočari-Industrial base seven kilometres away from Srebrenica

A note on pronunciation:

Č č=Ch

Ć ć-a softer Ch sound

Đ đ=softer Dj sound

Š š-Sh sound

Ž ž-Dj sound

J-is pronounced as Y, so *ašikovanje* is pronounced *ashikovanye.*

1-Silver Cross

1999

I stepped out of the cinema doors and blinked at the bright light blazing down from the undulating ceiling that was criss-crossed with square light boxes. Ninu took my hand as we walked and smiled at me, his chocolate brown eyes crinkling up in the corners, his dark hair gelled back. I knew he was imagining us together, his tanned skin against my white as we moved against each other. Lust coursed through my blood-stream, jump-starting my heart and making me feel alive. His jeans hugged his hips, and he wore a black t-shirt, a finger through the loophole of a black leather jacket over his shoul-der. He was a fine-looking specimen.

He gently lifted his hand and cupped my cheek, pressing his lips tenderly against mine. *Oh, no.* I detached my hand from his as we walked towards the stairs, my eyes glued to the red patterned carpet I was walking on, my copper wire eternity ring glinting on the ring finger of my right hand, a constant reminder of the price of love.

"I need to go to the bathroom, Phuong-Vy," I called when we reached the bottom of the stairs.

Phuong-Vy turned towards me, her black hair with purple streaks swaying, her blue eyes meeting mine. Looking into the bright blue-eyed contact lenses that hid her naturally brown eyes was disconcerting. She looked mysterious and slightly alien.

"Let's go to the bathroom," I nodded.

"I don't need to go," she said, hanging tighter onto the muscled arm of her new boyfriend Tom, the white singlet he wore emphasising his ropey physique. He was blonde and blue-eyed, his hair reaching his shoulders. Even though he was average height for a man, he loomed over Phuong-Vy, who barely reached 160 cm, in the high-heeled stilettos she'd paired with a red and white plaid mini skirt with knee-high socks and a white high-necked polo top. She looked adorable, a perfect mix of cute and sexy.

"Yes, you do." I gritted my teeth and grabbed her arm, marching her to the toilets at the back of the foyer.

Phuong-Vy pouted but said nothing, her short legs taking small, rapid steps to keep up with me.

"What's wrong, Seka?" she asked when we entered the bathroom, her Vietnamese accent cutting off the syllables in the words.

"I told you this was a bad idea," I said, pacing in front of the mirror.

"So what if he looks at you with puppy dog eyes?" Phuong-Vy stared at herself in the mirror as she used her finger to wipe the edge of her lipstick. "You don't owe him anything." She opened her handbag and rifled through, finding her lipstick.

I glared at her, fighting the urge to wrap my hands around her neck. When she'd suggested a couple's movie and dinner date night, I'd immediately said no. Going on double dates was a message I did not want to send to Ninu. We'd met on the job. I worked as a receptionist at a vet clinic, and he was the council ranger who came in sporadically to collect surrendered animals. We'd hooked up a few times, nothing serious, driving in his ute in the back streets to park on a dead-end road on the edge of the airport. The closest we'd come to a date was eating a pizza afterwards.

Phuong-Vy had worn me down. The date wasn't just any date; it was her birthday celebration. She'd lied to Tom that she was turning 21, the same age as me. She'd met Tom last weekend at a club and wanted to test if he was 'date ready' with a double date. Unlike me, she wasn't interested in random hookups without love and commitment; she was looking for the real deal. Now Ninu was getting the wrong idea—he thought we were in an actual relationship.

"Isn't Tom gorgeous. Those blue eyes, that blonde hair," she gushed.

"He's not my type." I looked at myself in the mirror and smoothed down my long brown hair, which was mussed.

"One of these days you'll have to tell me what you have against blondes?" Phuong-Vy said, handing me a brush. "What did you think of the movie?"

"It was good," I said, brushing my hair out. My jeans were loose, the pants fabric distressed with the knees cut out where I'd taken the scissors to them. My t-shirt was loose, but I'd tied the front into a knot, showing off my navel, my flannel shirt open over it. I'd purposely dressed down so Ninu would not think this was anything more than a movie catch up.

"It was so romantic when they did that parachute jump from the Eiffel Tower," Phuong-Vy said. We'd watched *French Kiss*, a rom-com featuring Meg Ryan and Kevin Kline.

"Yeah, sure." I handed her back the brush.

"I knew it. You didn't watch one bloody minute. There was no parachute jump. Maybe Ninu has the wrong idea because you couldn't keep your hands off him," Phuong-Vy said.

I glared at her. She smiled gleefully at me, her white teeth glinting in the fluorescent light against her tawny skin. I burst out laughing. She knew how to get me. My hormones always overpowered my good sense.

She took my arm and walked me to the bathroom door. "You just need to relax, enjoy tonight. Ride him good," she giggled as she opened the door.

Tom eyed Phuong-Vy hungrily as she walked towards him. I met Ninu's eyes. He watched me cautiously, like a feral cat deciding whether to trust a stranger.

"Are you okay?" he asked when I was at his side, his hands in his pockets.

"Yeah, great." I smiled, looking somewhere over his shoulder as I spoke.

Tom had his arm around Phuong-Vy's shoulder, his eyes on her cleavage as he looked down at her.

"Let's go to Chinatown for dinner," Phuong-Vy said. "I know the best restaurant."

We exited the double-storey glass doors and stepped under the awning jutting onto the footpath.

"Are you cold, babe?" Tom asked as Phuong-Vy shivered.

While it was a warm November day, now that it was later in the evening, there was a chill in the air. I don't know why he bothered asking, it's not like he was wearing a jacket he could lend her. He'd arrived in the singlet.

"I'm good. You keep me warm." Phuong-Vy tilted her head up, and he kissed her.

I resisted rolling my eyes as I took my jacket out of my backpack and shrugged it on. As I struggled with the sleeve, Ninu stepped forward, gently untangling it for me.

"Thank you," I murmured.

He nodded, not meeting my eyes. He looked like a wounded puppy. I don't know why I was being so churlish. I just needed to keep it light, the way Phuong-Vy said.

I put my arm through his and smiled at him. He smiled with relief. "I thought I did something wrong," he said.

"No, you're great." *Too great, and I don't want to hurt you.*

We followed Tom and Phuong-Vy a block and entered Chinatown through the large gate covered with a gold roof, the jade green pillars reaching the second floor of the buildings on each side where dragons were perched, red lanterns bobbing above us on each side of the street and casting a warm glow.

Phuong-Vy stopped suddenly, her foot awkwardly lurching as her heel caught in a drainage grate. Tom held her steady, and she didn't fall.

"My hero," she said, placing her hands on his chest and simpering.

I wouldn't have put it past her to be faking. As I watched them, the face from my nightmare appeared beside them. The thick black eyebrows above eyes so dark they looked black, the black hair I remembered as being dishevelled and long, now shorn short.

My stomach lurched, my skin breaking out in goose bumps as his craggy face took me back to that night of horror. Ninu was speaking next to me, but I couldn't hear anything he was saying. My heart hammered in my chest, lungs tight as I fought for breath, my legs weak. Could it really be him? The man was looking up and didn't see the woman who stopped suddenly in front of him, bumping into her. He smiled at her in apology, his hands holding her arm as she regained her balance, a gold tooth winking on his incisor. It was him. It was the bastard. Fear flooded my body, and my legs wobbled as I wilted.

"Seka," Ninu shouted as he held me up, his brown eyes crinkled with concern. "Are you okay?"

I opened my mouth to speak, but my chords were paralysed with fear. How to say the unspeakable?

Phuong-Vy tottered over to me. "You look like you're going to faint." Her icy hands gently touched my face, and as I met her fake blue eyes, I came back to earth with a thud. Which path do I follow? The path that led to my future, or back to my doomed past. My hands reached for the coin threaded through a necklace around my throat, and I rubbed the coin between my fingers.

"I have to go," I said, my vocal chords struggling to form sound.

I broke from her embrace and ran, my eyes searching for the dark-haired man wearing a blue shirt. He bobbed ahead in the crowd to my left, and I ran to catch up, blind to the entreaties and pleas of my friends. He was at the Bourke Street tram stop, and as the 96 tram pulled up, he waited for the doors to open before stepping onto the street and up the stairs. I threw myself up the stairs of the doorway closest to me, the doors shutting with a hiss behind me. As the tram sped up, I looked out the window and saw Ninu watching me from the street corner, frowning with confusion.

I turned away, walking down the middle of the aisle until I spotted the man. He was sitting on the right-hand side, his back to me, looking out the window. I sat on the opposite side of the aisle and watched him as we travelled down Bourke Street, turning onto Spring Street and passing Parliament House, before continuing down Johnstone Street and into Collingwood. Where was he going?

I shivered, clutching the silver coin commemorating Marshall Tito's death, 1892-1980, the second possession that I carried the day I left my home and became a refugee.

I was transported once again to three years before in the Potočari factory, the smell of death and decay permeating the surrounding air. The Serbs walked in packs, hunting for prey. The torchlight landed on me.

"What's that?" a gruff voice demanded, and hands yanked me to my feet. Rough hands grabbed the necklace at my throat, the chain cutting into the tender skin at the back of my neck.

His face was so close to mine that I smelled *rakija* as he breathed on me, a large silver cross dangling among the dark hair of his chest. "You're a genuine patriot," Silver Cross said, his finger rubbing the surface of the coin I had converted into a necklace, caressing President Tito's profile.

I looked into his soulless brown eyes, my back ached unwillingly towards him, the pressure from the necklace stopping me from stepping back. I knew better than to reply. You didn't provoke a beast in the wild.

"Is there any value there?" another Serb asked from behind him.

"No, just remnants of a dead nation," Silver Cross said, dropping the coin. "You can keep your silver, a reminder of your silver town long after you're gone from here."

As I swayed on the tram, I fought to breathe, hyperventilating. My mind jumped from one image to another.

I walked up to him, stabbing him with a knife to the chest, quickly, viciously, smiling as he fell to the ground, blood seeping from his wound.

I stood over him with a rock in hand, beating his head, crushing his skull as he moaned with pain.

I held a gun to his head, my finger on the trigger—

The image changed. Silver Cross stood behind Ramo, his finger on the trigger.

"Stop it," I muttered, slapping my head, pushing the thoughts away.

The woman across from me shifted in her seat, eyeing me nervously.

I looked back at Silver Cross; he was calmly in his own world, glancing out the window as we travelled down High Street while my blood was coursing through my veins like acid. I had to remain calm and not reveal who I was.

I practised the grounding exercise the counsellor had taught me. She called the 5 4 3 2 1 breathing. I looked out the window and counted with my fingers. The tram had stopped, and opposite was a large oak tree in the front yard of a house, the green leaves glistening in the sun. "I can see the tree outside the window," I held my thumb as I took a deep belly breath. The tram moved, and I looked back inside. Down the aisle was a baby in a pram. "I see the red balloon," I said, noting the string tied to the pram handle as I held my index finger and breathed out. "I see the feather." My eyes caught on a black straw hat with a purple feather tucked into the hatband as I moved to my middle finger, my breath calming my rapid heartbeat. "I see the yellow shirt," I stared at the man standing on the stairs as I held my ring finger. "I see the blue bike." I glanced out the window at a man racing the tram as I reached my pinkie finger.

I straightened my fingers, feeling calm descending. "I feel my feet on the ground. I feel my handbag." I touched the textured leather of the bag in my lap. "I feel the seat." I pressed my back against it. "I feel my jeans." I rubbed the fabric.

I tuned myself to the surrounding sounds, focusing on three sounds. "I hear the tram. I hear the motorbike. I hear the pedestrian crossing."

"I smell the perfume from the woman across from me. I smell the kebab the man a few seats down is eating."

"I taste popcorn," I remembered the popcorn I ate as I watched the movie.

As we neared the corner of Thornbury Village, he got up and stood near the door. When he stepped down the stairs at the back of the tram, I stood, heading for the door closest to me in the middle of the tram. He watched the street before he crossed, ignoring the pedestrian crossing two metres to the left. A car barely passed, and he launched onto the street. The oncoming car beeped, the driver gesticulating. Silver Cross continued walking as if the driver was invisible.

I walked to the pedestrian crossing and pressed the button. I wasn't going to do a Road Runner imitation for this bastard. Besides, he was walking slowly, so I could easily see him. He ducked into Psarakos, the shopping centre on the corner named after its Greek owners. I followed, looking at the dried fruit and nuts as I spotted him. He spent fifteen minutes decisively shopping. I collected some dried figs and weighed them. I went ahead of him and paid, then stood by the door, picking my figs as I waited for him to finish.

There was a Serbian newspaper on the stand beside me, and I impulsively bought it. It was written in Cyrillic, but having gone through the Yugoslav education system, I had alternated between the Latin script of English-speaking languages and the Cyrillic script created by a Serb linguist, Vuk Karadžić. The headline screamed:

***Men from Srebrenica Hiding in Plain Sight* by Dragica Milovanović**

The Bosnian Muslims claim that over 8,000 men and boys in Srebrenica were massacred and buried in mass graves, but this writer has found proof that this is Jihadist propaganda cooked up to gain international sympathy.

Radojka Živković, a former resident of Srebrenica who works as a cleaner, has seen her former neighbour, Zarif Avdić, on the streets of Melbourne. "I was catching the train home from the city after work. I got on the train at Flinders Street Station when I saw Zarif walking past the window. His wife claimed she was a widow, that her husband was lost and must be buried in mass graves, but there he was, healthy and hearty as the day I last saw him before I had to leave my beloved homeland."

Radojka is not the only person who has seen so-called victims alive and well. Nemanja Tomić said he spotted a former workmate from the tapestry factory they worked at in Chadstone Shopping Centre. "He was buying Reebok shoes at Shoe Warehouse. I called out to him, Zehrudin Hadžić, but he pretended not to know me. I know that our people would not have done this. It is not in our nature to be murderers, but it is the Balija's nature to murder and kill, that's what they've been doing since the Turk came and claimed our Serb kingdom and subjugated us."

This writer is collecting daily reports of more and more men claimed to have been killed in a fictional massacre, alive and well. In Germany, we have had numerous members of the Serb diaspora reporting seeing their former neighbours and workmates.

We will continue to exert pressure on the international community to stop promoting the ludicrous narrative that these men were bused from the Potočari Industrial Complex seven kilometres from the town of Srebrenica and then massacred. How many buses would it take to bus 8,000 + men? This lie is based on a ridiculous fallacy and has now been commemorated with a memorial built at Potočari with tombstones erected over empty graves to represent each one of these fictional deaths.

The international community must tell the truth—there was no massacre, there are no mass graves. Serbs are not the war criminals, it is in fact the Muslims who are blackening our names and committing war crimes by telling these lies.

My vision narrowed, and I balled the newspaper into my fist as rage coursed through my veins. These cowardly fuckers. They had committed massacre upon massacre, with mass graves being uncovered every day filled with broken bones from those they murdered, and yet they were playing the victim. I threw the newspaper into the rubbish bin, wanting to wash my hands of the filth attached to them.

I took deep breaths as the counsellor had instructed, calming myself until I regained composure. Once I was centred, I remembered my task and glanced around for Silver Cross. He had disappeared. In a panic, I dashed out of Psarakos and spotted his blue shirt further up the street. I hurried to catch up, relieved to see him walking slowly home with plastic bags swinging from his arms.

Silver Cross turned left. I reached the corner and saw he was gone. I ran up the street, eyeing the houses on the left-hand side he'd walked past—the front door closing on one house. I crossed the street and lurked behind a gum tree. The living room window had no curtains, and I saw Silver Cross walk through the room and into what must be the kitchen. He placed his shopping on the kitchen table and looked at the window. My heart stuttered to a stop. God, he saw me. He was coming to kill me.

He walked to the window and pulled the curtains closed.

I gasped with relief. I noted the number on his mailbox, 32, and looked at the street sign on the corner. David Street.

I've got you, you bastard.

I don't know how long I remained outside Silver Cross' house. Only when my teeth began chattering did I realise my legs and back were aching from standing in the same spot for so long. I was terrified he would disappear from my sight if I wasn't there to watch him. I breathed in and out, practising my grounding exercise, calming myself. He wasn't going anywhere. This was his home, and he didn't know I'd made him.

I walked to the tram stop, shivering. No trams were coming. I looked at my watch and realised it was after midnight. Public transport had stopped for the night. I spotted the orange NightRider sign for the buses that travelled during the early morning hours, providing safe passage to late-night revellers, and waited on the side of the road. Thankfully, the street was busy and well lit.

The bus arrived, and the doors opened before me.

"Are you okay, love?" the female bus driver asked as I stumbled on.

I nodded. I sat and looked out the window, seeing my reflection—no wonder the bus driver was concerned. I looked like I was a victim of a crime—my hair dishevelled, my eyes red, my face pale, shivering with shock. In a way, it was true, I was a victim of crime, it's just that the bruises and pain were internal.

The bus route ended in the city, and I walked another block to catch the NightRider to St Albans. The bus stopped at the train station, and I sighed and walked twenty minutes along Main Road East, past the high school, to Phuong-Vy's house. I opened the side gate and walked to the bungalow in the backyard, light seeping around the edges of the curtained windows even though it was 2 am.

I knocked gently on the window and called her name. Her front door opened, and she appeared wearing lavender silk pyjama shorts and a singlet, her hair loose around her shoulders.

"What happened?" she asked, quickly yanking me in and closing the door behind me.

"I saw the man who killed my father and fiancé," my teeth were chattering as I spoke.

2-Haunted

Phuong-Vy quickly rallied. "Shower first." She took my hand-bag off me and helped me take off my jacket. I clumsily attempted to undo my jeans, but my fingers felt thick. Phuong-Vy quickly helped me undress and wrapped a towel around me. She'd spent years caring for her mother, who had dementia and was well-versed as a caregiver.

Her bungalow was long and thin. We were in the kitchen and bathroom extension. There was a shower with a ceramic base surrounded by a shower curtain, opposite a long kitchen cupboard with a sink, and a kitchen table in the middle.

She deftly tied my hair up in a bun thanks to her years of experience as a hairdresser, then gently led me to the shower, opening the shower curtain and turning on the tap. She held her hand under the water until she was satisfied with the temperature. "Okay, step in." She took off the towel and folded it over the kitchen chair. "You okay?" she asked.

I nodded. She closed the curtain. The tension and fear left my body as the warm water sluiced over me. I cried for the first time since seeing Silver Cross, the sobs heaving from me. I heard Phuong-Vy puttering in the kitchen, but she didn't rush or interrupt me. She knew all too well that the only way to deal with pain was to let it wash over you in waves.

I turned off the shower. The curtain opened, and Phuong-Vy embraced me, wrapping a towel around me.

She started drying me, and I laughed. "It's okay, I can do it myself."

She smiled and handed me my pyjamas. I'd left my sleep-over bag at her place. Whenever we went out, I stayed at Phuong-Vy's place. Mama would not be happy with my nocturnal activities. She still needed to believe I was her untouched Bosnian girl, waiting for the wedding ring and certificate to give up my virtue. She didn't need to know that I had vowed never to marry or have children. War had taught me you had no control over life, and I wouldn't ever allow myself to be vulnerable again. If you don't love, you can't lose.

After I dressed, I followed Phuong-Vy up the stairs to the long room, which was her living room and bedroom. She'd used a cane screen to hide the bed and demarcate the two spaces. She was sitting on the armchair, and I sat on a two-seater sofa under the window. On the coffee table was a bowl of white rice with stir-fried vegetables and chicken on the side, a fork next to it. I'd attempted eating with chopsticks but was too impatient to learn. She urged me to eat as she poured us green tea from a teapot.

I didn't realise I was hungry until I saw the food and inhaled the chicken aroma. I served rice and stir-fry together and ate with a fork while Phuong-Vy patiently sipped her tea. Now that she was home, her energy was calm. It's like she put on a persona when she entered the world outside her home—with her fake blue contact lenses and brightly coloured hair clip-on extensions came the sparkly personality, but now she was all natural and the girl I first befriended three years before.

We had been new arrivals to Australia, learning English at the St Albans language school. She had been all natural, a typical Asian girl with waist-length black shiny hair, pale skin, and a scared look in her eyes. We had bonded over losing years of our lives—she was 29 years old, but looked so much younger.

She was the youngest of five siblings, a surprise when her Vietnamese parents thought their childbearing years were behind them. There was a ten-year gap between her and her next sibling. Her siblings had all married, a few moved away to live in Ho Chi Minh city, three of them emigrated to Australia, and so she was left to care for her elderly mother after her father's death when she was 12 years old. In the last few years, her mother had developed dementia, and she'd battled caring for her at home, attempting to piece together an income from sewing and money sent from her siblings living overseas.

When her mother passed away, she sold up everything she could and bought herself passage to Australia, travelling on a rickety boat—the only option available with her meagre funds. The trip had been long and dangerous. Pirates attacked the boat and stole the few trinkets the travellers had. Phuong-Vy lost her mother's pearl ring—the only thing she had of value. She never told me the specifics about what happened. All I knew was that there was a scar across her torso from a knife and that she'd spent months in a hospital recuperating from her injuries. I recognised the look in her eye as that of a woman who had suffered violence, the same look I had seen in the eyes of Bosnian women who were survivors of the rape camps.

I finished my *Banh mi* and collected the crumbs from my plate using my finger.

"What would you do to the men who hurt you?" I asked. "Like if you saw one of them walking the street. Would you want to hurt them back? Make them feel a little of the terror and pain you felt?"

Phuong-Vy stared thoughtfully at the wall in front of her. She shook her head. "I don't want to be who they are. I don't want to hurt them back."

"What? How can you say that?" I demanded, my hands fisting.

"I didn't always feel like this. I was angry when I went to the temple after I came to Australia. I wanted to hurt the men. Every night, I tossed and turned, my anger like fire burning me alive. I would fantasise about the most horrible ways of hurting them to get my revenge." Her eyes glinted with a remnant of that rage.

"I was losing weight, not getting better. The priest told me that Buddha says 'You will not be punished for your anger, you will be punished by your anger.' That's what was happening. My anger, not the men who hurt me, was punishing me. I had to change. I prayed every day, learning to forgive, and when I let go of my anger, I moved on."

Phuong-Vy nodded to the altar in the corner she'd made on a small coffee table, placing a photo of her parents with a vase of brightly coloured flowers, incense and a platter of oranges. Every morning, she lit incense and knelt before the altar to perform a prayer. Sometimes I woke and watched her from the coach, her face calm, the same tranquillity that my mother and brother exuded when they prayed as Muslims.

"You have to do the same, Seka. If you hold on to this rage, if you seek revenge, you will only be what this man is. You will become his hatred."

"How can you forgive such a monstrosity?" I demanded, my guts churning as I squeezed a cushion.

"I believe they will suffer karma and be punished."

"I don't believe in karma or God. That kind of faith eludes me. After what I had experienced in the war, I felt that God had abandoned this world long ago, leaving us trapped in chaos."

"You believe in justice. These war criminals are going to jail. You need to use that system and keep your hands and your conscience clean." Phuong-Vy pointed to the television. We'd watched the news last week featuring a report about the International Criminal Court that was in The Hague, Netherlands, where war criminals were going through the justice system and being jailed.

"But how do I go about getting him charged as a war criminal?" I had been so focused on wreaking pain and destruction that it hadn't even occurred to me that there were other avenues.

"You research. You call the police. You can find out. There is a system for everything in Australia, you just have to put in the work. You can do that."

I realised I knew someone—Alyssa Jones, the Australian journalist I had met and translated for while I was under siege in Srebrenica. She had been a war correspondent and was now travelling to The Hague to watch and write about the trials. She would know what to do.

I told Phuong-Vy about Alyssa. "I can track her down at the newspaper tomorrow at work."

"Good. You keep your thoughts pure. Buddha says, 'We are what we think. All that we are arises with our thoughts. With our thoughts, we make the world.' With your thoughts, you make justice, you make the world a better place by putting an evil man in jail. You don't think about anything else."

"You're right. I'll do that." I yawned, a wave of fatigue sweeping over me.

Phuong-Vy helped me up and quickly opened the sofa into a bed, placing bedding and pillows on it as I droopily watched her from the armchair.

"Tomorrow you have to call Ninu," Phuong-Vy said. "He was pretty down after you left. He left after you did."

I nodded, my mind shying away. I did not want to deal with that chestnut.

"How did it go with Tom?" I asked.

"Good." Phuong-Vy smiled like the cat who got the cream. "He was a consummate gentleman. He brought me home and kissed me at the door. Didn't try to come in."

"Wow," I arched my eyebrows. "That's great."

Phuong-Vy smiled with delight. "This might be the one. This might be my Mr Darcy."

She'd been reading *Pride and Prejudice*, a novel she'd loved in Vietnamese and was now re-reading in English to improve her language skills. She was obsessed with Austen's world of social propriety and matches that were all about marriage. I worried about her romantic outlook, but couldn't say anything. She was a 29-year-old virgin and was saving herself for marriage. She'd spent most of her life being her mother's carer and now wanted to have her own family.

Her sister had attempted to set her up with eligible men in the community, but they were all older and either widowed or divorced, often with children from previous marriages. "They're not seeking a wife. They're looking for a babysitter," she said. She was determined not to be burdened with caring for others again. She desired an Australian husband, hoping it would offer her more freedom and less adherence to traditional expectations. Moreover, she wanted to have her own child, just one. Growing up in a family plagued by poverty, she wanted a brighter future for her offspring.

"I hope Tom is the one," I said, pulling her into a tight hug. "He'd be lucky to have someone as amazing as you."

Phuong-Vy rubbed my back. "Me too."

I lay down, and she covered me. I heard her padding to the bed behind the screen and fell asleep hard.

I lay on a jacket on the cold concrete floor, my legs rubbing on the rough surface where the jacket ended. I heard creaking and opened my eyes. Above me was the sawtooth factory ceiling, crisscrossed with beams. A doll hung from one beam by a rope, creaking as it swung. I looked closer. It was a young girl hanging by the neck, blonde hair trapped in the rope, her face purple and swollen, dried blood visible from under her torn dress and on her legs. Fear choked me, turning my body to jelly as her blue eyes stared at me sightlessly, pinning me in place.

Suddenly, the concrete floor vanished, and I was in a field littered with skulls. The blonde girl was on the ground at my feet—she decomposed before my eyes, her skin turning blue, then grey, flaking away and falling off, leaving nothing but her skeleton. I tried running but felt laden and heavy, as if trapped in mud. As I stepped, the crunching sound of a crushed skull echoed beneath my feet. Glancing down, I saw my foot had crushed her skull, and her skeleton was sinking into the mud, pulling me under.

The field vanished, and I was lying in a pit of dead bodies, a bright light above me. People were kneeling on the edge above me. *Pop, pop* and bodies fell into the pit, covering me. The blonde girl landed on top of me, her body crushing me so I couldn't breathe, her blue eyes staring into mine. My scalp prickled, the hairs on the back of my neck stood up as bulldozers began pushing earth on top of me, burying me alive. I tried wriggling and grunting with exertion, but something pinned my arms to my side.

Two arms reached for me into the pit, moving the girl off me, lifting me out of the pit.

"You're okay, Seka. You're safe." Arms clasped me. I opened my eyes and saw Phuong-Vy's face above mine, her black hair tickling my face. She was on the sofa bed with me, my torso across her lap as she rocked me.

"I couldn't help her. I couldn't help any of them," I cried, waves of guilt crashing over me. Why did I survive when so many died? If I hadn't gotten my period that night in Potočari, it might have been me the Serbs took away and raped. I might have been the one who swung from the rope rather than live with the horror.

"I know." Phuong-Vy caressed my hair as I trembled, fear coursing through me.

My throat hurt and I realised I must have been screaming. "I'm thirsty."

Phuong-Vy helped me sit up and brought me a glass of water. I gulped it down, my mouth bone dry. I must have been screaming for a while. Phuong-Vy returned with a damp cloth and gently bathed my face.

I was so tired, my body ached, and my head throbbed. I closed my eyes, then jerked awake, too scared to sleep.

"It's okay. I'm here." Phuong-Vy lay under the doona with me. She put her arm under the pillow and let me curl against her. "You're safe now."

I glanced at her; she was staring at the ceiling, tears seeping from her eyes. "I'm sorry," I said, touching her wet cheeks. She had suffered her own night terrors, but in the past few months had enjoyed a peaceful sleep, and now I was burdening her with mine.

"This is our refugee baggage. We carry it every day." She stroked my back, soothing me to sleep. "Tonight I will keep you safe from the hungry ghosts."

Phuong-Vy called the dead spirits who haunted us hungry ghosts. They were souls who had not received a proper burial and so haunted the living, searching for recognition. We had spent many a night being sentinels guarding the other from the darkness of our past. I wondered if I would ever again know a peaceful night, or if haunting dreams would forever plague me.

3-Photo

I waited in the coffee shop, twirling a serviette in my hands. Alyssa Jones walked past the glass window, her shoulder-length black hair loose around her face. It had been three years since I saw her in Tuzla airport when I was a refugee, where my mother, brother, and I shared a tent as we waited for a visa to come through for Australia.

Alyssa stepped into the cafe and scanned it with her dark eyes crinkling around the corner. Her father, an Australian National Serviceman, was conscripted into the Vietnam War, where he met her mother. Alyssa inherited her mother's Asian eyes and her father's freckled Anglo nose.

She saw me and walked towards me with a smile. I had changed little. I was filled out more, and my hair was long again. I'd cut it while we were in the refugee camp, but I could not keep it clean. Three years of war, rationing, and starvation in Srebrenica left me emaciated and pale before our expulsion. I now looked like any other 22-year-old Australian girl, pink-cheeked with good health, curvy and womanly. I'd had multiple oral surgeries to repair the rotten teeth from my wartime diet and could now smile again, even though there was nothing to smile about.

Alyssa approached, kissing me on the cheek. "Salam Aleikum," she said the Arabic phrase of peace be upon you.

"Aleikumu Salam," I returned the greeting, peace be upon you.

She'd spent many times in Bosnia and was used to our customs. I met her when I was 15, and I translated for her at Srebrenica Hospital, enduring medieval surgeries performed on shelled and shot patients without anaesthetic while Alyssa reported to obtain international aid. The international community didn't save my people, but Alyssa had spent the six years in between writing about the war, refugee experiences and now about the War Tribunal.

"How long have you been in Australia?" she asked, sitting.

"Three years." I caught her up on my studies. My lifelong dream was to be a veterinarian. I was now in my first year of university.

A waitress approached, and we ordered coffees.

"I'm so glad you've picked up where you left off," Alyssa said.

"Yes, four years later," I said bitterly. When we came to Australia, I first completed an English language course, then high school at an adult learning centre, and now university. I wouldn't finish the seven years of undergraduate and post-graduate studies required to be a vet until I was 30. The war had stolen more than my fiancé and father—it had stolen years off my life.

"How is your family?" she asked.

"Mama is working as a cleaner. It was the only job she could get because her English is rudimentary." My mother had been an administrator in our homeland, working in the factory where my father was an engineer, dressing every day in pretty dresses and wearing red lipstick. Now she cleaned high-rise buildings with a Bosnian cleaning crew. Her back hurt, and her hands were rough and dry from the cleaning product. She looked much older than her 45 years with her hair grey and her face creased from grief and pain.

"Emir works at an assembly line factory. He's studying part-time and hopes to get into the designing department." My brother wanted to be an engineer like our father, but at 25 years old, he had given up on that dream. We needed his salary to keep us fed and housed. Instead, he was completing a trade course in Computer Aided Drafting, hoping to get a job in the design department of the car factory where he worked.

"I brought something for you. After you emailed me, I went back through my archives and found this." She slid a photo across the table.

I gasped when I saw Ramo in the photo. I didn't have a picture of him. His likeness only existed in my mind since I last saw him. The UN had arrived, bringing in a food aid convoy, journalists with them eager for news. Ramo and I had followed the convoy to the textile factory, desperate for food. In the photo, we were standing side by side, he was slightly in profile, glancing at me, the textile factory in the background. His blonde hair glinted in the sun, his blue eyes hidden in shadow, but I remembered how blue they were. He was looking at me, a softness on his face, his love apparent. Fifteen-year-old me stared hard at the camera, my face narrow and pale from malnourishment, daring the world to care about us.

I reached out, gently tracing his face as tears flowed down my face.

"Have they found him?" Alyssa asked.

Bodies were being exhumed from mass graves daily. Emir went to the Melbourne Bosnian embassy to submit his DNA; this would allow for a match if our father's remains were found. I had been in touch with Ramo's mother, Edina, who had submitted her DNA. She now lived in Sarajevo and campaigned with a women's group she'd helped establish, the Mothers of Srebrenica, fighting to recognise the massacre and international aid. She and the other mothers successfully got a memorial built at Potočari to bury the massacre victims. They erected tombstones inscribed with each victim's name, to be laid to rest when their remains were found.

I shook my head, hugging the photo to my chest. I was back in Potočari, the industrial complex that Srebrenicians had fled to seeking shelter as Serb forces attacked the town, sure in the knowledge that the UN, which had declared the city a Safe Zone, would use air bombs to repel the enemy. Instead, we'd spent three days sleeping on concrete floors, enduring torture and rape, as we waited for the Serbs to make their final move. As the Serbs led us to the buses, it was a beautiful summer day, the green fields around us shimmering in the warm breeze.

I'd felt Ramo's hand gently touching my hair, his whisper tickling in my ear as he told me not to worry. The Serb soldier who pushed him away from the bus doors as he tried to climb in lied and told me he would be exchanged for another prisoner. I knew in my heart that it would be the last time I saw him. He remained frozen in time, his golden hair distinct among the other men being led to their slaughter, as he walked to his certain death. Three years earlier, Serbs had taken his father and three brothers from a different bus as they tried to escape their village, slaughtering them on the roadside while Ramo and his mother drove away. His youth saved him then. On 11 July 1995, in Potočari, he was 19 years old and out of miracles.

"I'm sorry," Alyssa said. "It's so hard for the survivors left behind. So, what did you come and see me about?" Alyssa asked.

"You've been reporting on the Criminal Tribunal," I said.

Like all Bosnians, I was following the newspaper reports about the war crimes that were being judged in the International Criminal Tribunal for the former Yugoslavia (ICTY). The Tribunal was a United Nations court of law established to deal with war crimes that took place during the Bosnian War. The United Nations created it in 1993, during the war, after witnessing the atrocities perpetrated by the Serbs; yet, even with this proof, they left Srebrenica alone and undefined in 1995, when the greatest massacre on European soil since World War II occurred, according to my newspaper reading. I found it to be a remarkable irony that when World War II ended with the Holocaust, the world had vowed never to let the same thing happen again. Yet genocides keep happening all around the world, in Rwanda, in Srebrenica, in Cambodia. We never learned.

Alyssa nodded. The waitress brought out coffees and placed them in front of us.

"How is a war criminal arrested?" I asked.

Her eyes narrowed with curiosity, but she didn't ask. "The Tribunal has collected testimonies from survivors since its establishment. Consequently, the Tribunal has recorded the names of the perpetrators and the victims. They give some witnesses an alias to protect their anonymity." She stirred the sugar into the coffee. "Once sufficient evidence exists, the prosecutor requests an arrest warrant or a voluntary summons, so the suspect's country of residence must arrest and extradite them to the Netherlands."

"Is that why so many of them are hiding in Serbia?" I demanded.

Alyssa nodded as she licked the foam off her spoon and placed it on the saucer. "A lot of Serbs are true patriots and are hiding them."

"What if they're in Australia?" I asked.

"Australia is a signatory to the UN Charter and will extradite war criminals."

"Doesn't it take years for someone to go through the court system?" I'd read about a war criminal who committed crimes in 1992 in Omarska, the Bosnian concentration camp where people suffered torture in the most foul manner. They indicted him in 1995, and five years later, his case was undergoing appeal.

"Yes, justice moves slowly, but it does move. And with each war criminal indicted, victims receive more information about their missing relatives," Alyssa said.

I fingered the piece of paper in my handbag, unsure whether or not to hand it over. Before meeting Alyssa, I had retraced my steps to Silver Cross' house, wanting to make sure that everything I saw wasn't a figment of my imagination. As I watched his house from across the street, a postie rode up, placing envelopes in the mailbox built into the brick fence. The wad was thick and didn't drop into the mailbox; instead, it remained hanging out onto the street. A dog barked from the backyard, and I saw its muzzle as it pushed through the hole in the gate at the side of the house. I waited to see if anyone would emerge to go to the mailbox, but all remained quiet on the suburban street. The postie rode his bike around the corner, but no one else appeared on the street.

Seeing my chance, I walked past Silver Cross' house, my hand snatching the envelopes jutting out as I continued walking, the dog's barks following me down the street. My shoulders tensed as I waited for someone to shout or chase me. The dog stopped barking, and quiet descended. I went to the tram stop and looked at the envelopes. They were bills, a water bill, and junk mail for the residents of the house. I read his name *Miroslav Vlahović*. Miroslav—an ironic name in this instance, as it translated to Peaceful Slav, and yet he was anything but peaceful. He had looted and terrorised Bosnian refugees at Potočari and then helped massacre thousands.

I dropped the letters into the red mailbox near the bus stop. The post office would re-deliver them, and Silver Cross would be none the wiser about what I did. As I travelled on the tram, I wrote all the information I had collected about Silver Cross for Alyssa, including witnessing the atrocities he committed at Potočari. I now hesitated about handing it over. It was out of my hands once I gave this information to Alyssa. The path to justice would trundle slowly. Could I endure the years it would take to bring him to justice? Wasn't it better to exact my pound of flesh and practice an eye for an eye?

"The best way to flush these criminals out is to write about them. Collect evidence from as many witnesses as possible and publicise them. Then more witnesses will come forward, and they will be arrested," Alyssa said.

I remembered Phuong-Vy's advice: *If you hold on to this rage, if you seek revenge, you will only be what this man is.* I had to think about the bigger picture. The more criminals who went through the justice system, the more it would help victims.

I handed over the piece of paper. Alyssa looked down as she read. A minute later, she looked up thoughtfully.

"Miroslav Vlahović," she said his name. "I'll contact my sources at the Tribunal and see if his name came up in witness testimonies. Do background research about him. The Tribunal will send a representative to interview you and your family, collect witness statements. When the story is solid, we publish. The more pressure we bring, the quicker he'll get indicted."

"What can I do?" I asked.

"Nothing. You don't want to tip him off that someone knows about his history. He might leave, go underground, and then become untraceable. We need to work in secret, remaining hidden until the trap is set."

I nodded.

"Promise?" Alyssa asked.

I nodded.

She squeezed my hand. "We'll get him Seka. Trust me."

A weight had dropped from my shoulders. It was now out of my hands. Alyssa was the one who would take on this job.

Alyssa stood and placed her handbag over her shoulder. "Did you ever get in touch with your friend Zora?" Alyssa asked.

The last time we saw each other, Alyssa had passed on a letter from my best friend Zora. We'd grown up together, our houses side by side, our fathers' best friends, thinking we were one people—Yugoslavs. And then the war arrived in our small mountain town, and we were now Serb and Bosnian, on opposite sides of a war that we didn't believe in or want.

I shook my head.

"Oh, well, if you ever do, I'd love to write about it."

I watched her walk out of the cafe with purpose and resolve.

4-Picnic

Mama turned into the driveway of the mosque, the white domed building and tower looking like a fairytale castle. In Srebrenica, the Cryer, climbing the minaret, would fill the air with the Arabic call to prayer, summoning the faithful to prayer; however, in this suburban setting, the minaret served only as decoration.

I got out of the car and hesitated. "Come on," Mama urged.

I sighed and followed. The Bosnian community funded the mosque, and the Imam organised picnics for Bosnian families to mingle and see the mosque's progress. They would then be motivated to donate when they saw the lists of donors on noticeboards in the mosque, and with the Bosnian community radio station also reading out donor names. Since the mosque was built with a kitchen to prepare food, there was no further need for picnics, but the name stuck to the community gatherings on its site.

A woman greeted Mama as we walked through the car park. "My daughter Seka," Mama said, putting her hand on my back and pushing me forward. Next to the woman was a young Bosnian man, a few years older than me. He gave me a quick once-over and looked away.

"My son Haris," the woman said.

Mama and the woman walked ahead of us, leaving Haris and me to small talk, turning their heads to check we were engaging. This was the reason I hated attending these community events. My mother and her friends viewed it as a meat market that was just about parading young Bosnian men and women together to make a match. The only thing they were interested in was ensuring the continuity of the culture.

"What do you do for a job?" I asked.

"Concreting with my father."

I waited for him to ask a question in return, but silence greeted me. These arrogant asshole Bosnian men.

"So you got a *Vlah* girlfriend, then?" I asked, purposely being rude by using the derogatory slur for non-Muslim.

He jerked, quickly looking ahead to see if his mother had heard. "What makes you say that?"

I knew his type. He would date every nationality he could, sowing his wild seeds while playing the dutiful son, then find some Bosnian import to marry who would stay home while he continued his life as if he were still single.

I dashed away, leaving him behind me.

"Seka, Seka," Mama called, but I refused to turn around.

She caught up with me in the toilet. "What happened to that nice young man?"

"He's not nice, and he's not someone I give a shit about. Try to do that again, and I'll walk home," I shouted.

"Keep it down," Mama hissed, grabbing my arm. "They don't all need to hear our business."

"Then stop this shit."

"Okay, okay," Mama held her hands up in surrender.

When we returned, she introduced me to her friends, talking about my veterinarian degree and my job at the vet clinic. Now she was doing the second most famous thing these picnics were good for, bragging about her offspring. It was like watching two cowboys walking out onto High Street at noon, eyeing each other as they prepared to engage in battle, except it was middle-aged women in billowing scarves and loose chiffon skirts and blouses, competing in who could out-boast each other in their children's accomplishments.

Mama greeted another woman. Her daughter was with her, wearing a hijab. She'd married an Afghan and wore it according to the customs of their culture. The only way it was permissible to be married out of the Bosnian community was if it was to another Muslim ethnicity.

I nodded at a friend I knew from language school. She was wearing a hijab too, but it wasn't her choice. After the war, her father converted and insisted that all the women in his family wear hijabs, even though it was never part of our Bosnian culture. Only older women wore headscarves, and that was more for practicality to keep their long hair tucked away, rather than modesty. Her father and brothers were next to her, wearing t-shirts, and the teenage son wore shorts. These men wanted to gain bonus points for their religious fervour at the expense of the women's right to choose how they wanted to dress. Muslim custom dictates that he should also dress modestly, covering all limbs, just like the women. But that part of the *hadiths*, decrees by the Prophet Mohammed, always went unspoken. The women always carried the burden. The hypocrisy grated on me.

I saw Adnan and smiled for the first time since we arrived. His father also disappeared in Srebrenica. There were a handful of us from Srebrenica, and we always gravitated towards each other. Even in this small community, our missing family members made us outliers, leaving an unseen but ever-present void.

"They found him," Adnan said. "They found my father." His eyes were glistening with unshed tears.

My stomach lurched, a strange mix of happiness and jealousy. "Where?"

"They found his femur in a mass grave in Glogova. They asked us if we wanted to wait to see if they recovered more of his body or return this summer to have him buried."

"Oh, wow," I said, tears seeping from my eyes, even as I fought to contain them.

"We're going back to Srebrenica this July for the funeral at the Potočari memorial."

"I'm so happy for you." I hugged him. I tried to hold back the tears, but I couldn't. As I held him, I cried, the sobs breaking through.

"It's okay. Let it out." He hugged me tightly. "They'll find your father and Ramo. I know they will."

I nodded, wanting to believe. I stepped away from Adnan and got a tissue from my handbag. "Have you got any family over there?"

He shook his head. "We're going through Sarajevo and then will get a bus to Srebrenica. A neighbour, Fatima, has returned and we're staying with her." Adnan ruffled his hair. "She told me my best friend also returned to Srebrenica."

Adnan and I had spent many hours talking about our life before the war. We both had best friends who were Serbs.

"Are you going to catch up with him?"

Adnan looked at me, his eyes pooling with pain. "How can I? How can I speak to him knowing that his people did that to my father?"

"We won't be wasting our spit on any Serbs," his mother butted in. "They've all got blood on their hands."

I nodded. This was always the message: keep away from Serbs. They were our enemy. They were the ones who were responsible for the death of our menfolk, for losing our homes, even if they weren't there or did anything. I sometimes wondered, weren't we perpetuating the same hate that got us here? What would happen in 20 years when another generation grew up without the memory of the war? Would they harbour the same hatred and ideas that led us to this point?

We used to be one people, mingling together. I remembered my father's belief in brotherhood and unity. I didn't let myself travel too far down this road, thinking about what my life might have been like if the genocide hadn't happened, wondering who I would be?

I'd be with Ramo on his land. Under the warm Bosnian sun, the green undulating valley spread out before us. I would be studying in Sarajevo and returning home for holidays, and when I finished, we would get married. I would still be able to become a veterinarian and live with him. Our lives would be together, always. Instead, I was living under the burning Australian sunshine that leeched the colour from the landscape.

Mama and I said goodbye to Adnan and sat at a table. I saw Emir with a group of his friends. Each of them was bearded, wearing loose jeans or pants and shirts that satisfied the modesty requirement of Muslims. They were setting up the tables and chairs for everyone to eat after prayer. He was the perfect Muslim—he volunteered at the mosque regularly and came every Friday for prayers.

When the call to prayer was called, men who could pray drifted to the washrooms to take *abdest* and perform ablutions by washing themselves before their prayers. The women followed, going into the women's room. Afterwards, the men and women were segregated—the men entered the main mosque on the ground floor while the women climbed the narrow stairs on the side of the mosque to the balcony where women prayed. A few women who couldn't climb the stairs went to the downstairs prayer room at the back of the room.

"Come on," Mama beckoned.

"No, I'm unclean," I said.

The *hadith* declared that menstruating women were unclean, forbidden from prayer until their menses had passed. Mama shot me a suspicious look but said nothing. I was lying. Every time we came to the mosque, I suddenly had my period. I never prayed. I wanted to believe in God, I really did—but the harder I tried, the more impossible it felt. I could almost see my father, watching the faithful hurry to their prayers, his mouth curled in scorn.

Most Bosnians in the mosque had been Communist party members, relinquishing religious practice in Bosnia to gain system benefits, promotions, and company apartments given to those with connections. But now they were all devout religious sheep, after they realised the Serbs hated and wanted to kill them, no matter how watered down their faith was.

My waning faith disappointed my mother and brother. They believed we were all the chosen ones. We could have each of us died hundreds of times in a hundred different ways during the three-year siege of Srebrenica, and yet we didn't. My brother had survived seven days of trekking across the Bosnian countryside in the Death March as Serbs rounded up Bosnian boys and men to be massacred.

I didn't feel chosen. I had survived, but I had left my heart and soul in Bosnia, in Ramo's unmarked grave. Even though I knew I should be lucky to be here in Australia, living the dream that he never got to live, everything felt fake and unreal. I felt like an actor playing the humble refugee grateful for asylum in this bountiful country, yet I remained tethered to my homeland, my blood calling to the blood spilled there.

When I'd tried speaking to Mama or Emir about this, they told me this would pass. For them, it was easy, surrender to faith and belief. For me, not that simple. How did God decide to spare some of these corrupt motherfuckers, who thrived on Communist propaganda, while my Ramo died and was buried? How did some of these assholes live, who drank alcohol and beat their wives, while my father didn't?

It was all fucking random. Just one big trick. There was no mystery or reason. When I'd gone to see a counsellor, she told me I was suffering from survivor's guilt. She said that I felt like I did something wrong for surviving when others didn't, and I was trying to punish myself. That this was why I engaged in self-destructive behaviour. I didn't believe her. This wasn't self-destruction—it wasn't about punishment. I just needed to feel something, anything. For years, I had clung to a dream of a life with Ramo, a life that never happened. I refused to keep living in that illusion. It was time to exist, to stop pretending.

I settled into a chair in the common room next to the kitchen. A few women sat huddled around the tables—other 'unclean' ones on their periods. Unlike me, I doubted any of them were faking. I pulled out my textbook, lifting my backpack onto my lap. Over time, I had perfected the art of shutting down small talk—nothing killed conversation faster than playing the role of the dutiful student.

I went to the toilet and walked past the entrance to the prayer room, where there was a Mihrab, a niche showing the direction of Mecca that all Muslims prayed to. All the men rose and fell in unison, praying silently. There was beauty and elegance in their movements. I could see the vibration of their prayers and thoughts travelling towards God. Could he hear them? Would he protect them and give them succour now in this country?

As I watched, tears welled in my eyes. I heard Ramo's voice in my ear. "There is no God. There is only now."

Whenever I attempted to pray, my mind wandered from me, setting me off down dangerous terrain. Invasive thoughts took hold, memories of Srebrenica, of pain, deprivation, blood and screaming. It was like the more silent and still I was, the more the pain burrowed inside. I needed to keep moving.

I returned to the recreation room near the kitchen, settled at the table, and opened my book. If there was one thing I excelled at, it was silencing my thoughts. I slipped on my Walkman, let the music fill my head, and focused on the pages before me.At some point, Mama appeared with a plate of *ćevapi*—skinless beef sausages nestled in thick Turkish bread, with a side of minced onion and a soft drink. I picked at the food absentmindedly, highlighting passages as I chewed. Time blurred. At some point, the empty plate and cup vanished, whisked away without me noticing.

Someone shook my shoulder, and I looked up, realising it was Mama. The recreation room was once again full of people. I had been sitting there for hours after the prayers had finished and my mother and brother socialised, alone in my company and content.

I packed up my books and followed them to the car, glad to leave the mosque and its tortured walls behind.

I lay in bed reading. I'd attempted to sleep for two hours, tossing and turning as I battled insomnia, feeling like ants were walking on my skin as I scratched my flesh, leaving red marks on my skin. My eyes kept drifting from the pages of my novel to the framed photo of me and Ramo. I took it to K-Mart, had them scan and crop it, enlarging our faces, and then put it in a wooden frame on my bedside table. As I looked at his face, I closed my eyes and saw him crystal clear in my memories again, his blue eyes looking at me, the blonde stubble on his skin like golden sprinkles shimmering on his skin. He had been so beautiful and perfect at 19 years old, forever frozen in the prime of his life. Even though we were locked in Srebrenica under siege, I had dreamed of a life beyond the mountain peaks that held us prisoner; yet now that I was free, I could barely see tomorrow.

I heard a noise and lowered my book, listening. It sounded like a trapped animal. I ran from my bed, threw open my bedroom door, and entered Emir's bedroom. He was lying in bed on his back, his body arched as if he were in agony.

"Emir, Emir, wake up," I urged, grabbing his shoulders as I yanked him from his night terrors. He screamed even more as he fought to rouse himself from his demons. "You're okay. You're safe." I gently stroked his face, urging him to wake up.

His eyes fluttered open. For a moment, he looked disoriented, his face full of terror, before his body went limp in surrender. "I'm okay," he said, opening his eyes fully.

I snapped the lamp open beside him, and he flinched. His bedroom was sparse, with a bed and desk, and only a tapestry of the mosque at Mecca hanging on the wall.

"Do you want hot chocolate?"

He sat up and nodded.

"I'll meet you in the kitchen." I closed his bedroom door behind me as I left. I heard him sobbing behind me. He hated anyone seeing him cry, so I'd learned to give him his privacy.

He came in as I was warming the milk on the stove. "Is Mama home?"

I shook my head.

Emir walked over to the answering machine. "Children," Mama's voice rang out. "I got overtime and won't be home until 3 am. I'll see you tomorrow. Love you."

Emir deleted the message. Mama took every night shift she could. We had sold our house in Srebrenica to a Serb family while in Australia, and received just enough money so that we could put down a deposit on a three-bedroom yellow brick house in St Albans that was built in the 1950s with screw top windows and mould in the bathroom. Mama was determined to rid herself of the mortgage and took every shift she could to put extra repayments on and undertake renovations.

I added the cocoa to the boiling milk and stirred it before pouring it into two mugs. The kitchen hadn't been updated since the 1970s with yellow laminate cupboards and a green-tiled countertop. I placed the saucepan into the sink, ran warm water through it, and took the mugs into the living room. Emir was sitting on the couch, staring blankly at the television screen we'd bought second-hand, and sitting in an empty wall cabinet that was a donation. Mama bought knick-knacks from the op shop, one at a time, savouring the experience of shopping to decorate. We had two photos on display of our life in Srebrenica. One was a photo of my father holding Emir as a baby, which he'd sent to his cousin in Germany. The cousin had reproduced it, and we had a faded copy. The second photo was of my parents' wedding day, she'd sent to my uncle Mustafa. There were a few photos my uncle had reproduced from our trip to Australia when I was a child, but my father was at a conference or taking the photos, so we had no other images of my father.

The TV show Rage was playing, a music video show hosted by an Australian musician who selected their favourite songs every week.

I handed Emir the mug. It took him a moment to notice and take it from my hand.

"Bad dreams again?" I asked. I had been looking for the right moment to tell him about seeing Silver Cross, but this wasn't the right moment. His memories already tormented him enough.

"I was on the Death March. We were marching through the woods when gas filled the air. All the men around me turned into monsters with monster heads and began attacking each other. I crawled on the ground until I could run away." He spoke like a robot, as if the nightmare still held him in its thrall.

During the Death March, Serbs hunted 10,000 Bosnian men like prey as they embarked on a deadly seven-day trek through the forest. Serbs dressed in stolen UN uniforms and impersonated UN soldiers so that Bosnian men surrendered. They released poison gas, which made Bosnian men hallucinate and turn on each other. Only 3,000 Bosnians survived the trek. Emir hardly ever spoke about what he had endured. Only on nights like this, when he was in the twilight between the past and present, he revealed bits and pieces of his harrowing survival.

"Did you hear about Adnan?" he asked, sipping his hot chocolate while music played in the background.

I nodded. It was always a lightning rod when someone found their relatives and could bury them.

"I keep wondering if we'll ever find Babo."

"Me too," I whispered, my throat tight.

"I wish there was some way we could make it happen. I would kill to find the truth. Sometimes in my dreams I'm back in the army. We're hunting the Serbs." Emir had learned to hunt in the country when we visited our grandparents and was a skilled marksman. "I notched up five kills. In my dreams, I'm re-living my kills, shooting them in the head, one after the other, killing them. Sometimes my trigger finger itches." He lifted his hand, miming sighting a rifle. "I just want to kill them all."

My skin broke out in goose pimples at the venom in his voice. He had never told me about the soldiers he'd killed.

"That was war. You could kill to protect yourself. If you did that now, you'd end up in jail."

He smiled grimly. "And happily too. I would be a true martyr for the cause." His eyes glowed with malice, as if I were talking to a stranger.

"You can't talk like that. If you ended up in jail, it would destroy Mama and me." I took his hand, trying to bring him back to the present. "This is not what Allah wants."

"I don't care. I would burn a thousand times in pits of hell if I could take one bastard with me."

"You're not thinking this through. You're a person of faith. You need to hold onto it—it will give you strength. Let's pray." I took his hand and began reciting the Arabic prayers I had memorised. His fingers tightened around mine as he closed his eyes, murmuring the words with fervent devotion. Slowly, his grip loosened. The tension in his face softened, the pain etched into his features easing as he lost himself in the rhythm of prayer.

We prayed as our hot chocolate cooled and congealed, the cold seeping into my bones, but I didn't stop. I was fighting to save my brother's soul, to bring him back from the brink of despair. His prayers started slowing, and he yawned.

"It's time for bed," I said, helping him to stand from the couch. I led him to his bedroom and helped him lie down, covering him with a doona. I left the night light on as I left his bedroom.

As I washed the mugs and saucepan, I realised I could never tell my brother about Silver Cross. Emir was fighting to hold onto his sanity under the weight of his memories of the war.

If he knew about Silver Cross, it might tip him over to revenge and a path he could never walk back from.

I made tea and a grilled cheese sandwich and was eating it when Mama walked through the front door at 4 am.

"What are you doing up?" she asked as she took her shoes off in the hallway.

"Emir had a nightmare."

Mama nodded and tiptoed to his bedroom, peering in. "He's sleeping peacefully now," she said when she returned. She sat at the dining table with a sigh, sipping her peppermint tea as she ate.

"He told me he killed five men when he was in the army." I held my hands around my teacup, warming them.

Mama slowed her chewing, then swallowed and took a sip of tea.

"I think he needs to talk to someone about what happened. Get some counselling." I'd taken part in counselling when we first arrived in Australia. The counsellor had diagnosed me with PTSD. She'd said it was common for survivors of a significant trauma like war and violence to only process their emotions when they were in a safe environment. Mama had never talked about her memories of war. It's like she just buried her memories in a little box in her head and never went back there. Emir had tried counselling, but quickly stopped as it set off his nightmares. He'd devoted himself to faith instead and claimed this was his treatment.

"It's in the past. It does no good to dwell on terrible memories," Mama said.

"I'm worried about him. It's like he's being torn apart by what happened."

"We just need to focus on tomorrow. Be grateful for what we have and we'll be fine." Mama got up and took her cup and plate to the sink. "You need to get some sleep. You have to work in the morning."

I sighed and went to my bedroom. I lay on my bed and touched my photo, imagining touching Ramo's face. My brother had to devote himself to faith in order to live. My mother had to sink into denial, while I had to focus on justice to survive. I would work with Alyssa alone to bring Silver Cross to justice. This was my salvation.

5-Fluke

I walked into the vet clinic with relief. Keisha, the receptionist, was mopping the reception floor—the odours of cat urine
and pine and vinegar disinfectant battling each other.

I nodded hello to Mrs Jenkins. She'd been coming for a year
with her cat, Mr Tingles. They looked alike with their long
faces and fluffy white hair. Mrs Jenkins was watching Keisha
guiltily. Mr Tingles' incontinence was not getting any better.

I went behind the counter and to the kitchenette, placing
my lunch in the fridge. Mama made me cheese pita, and
just thinking about it made my stomach rumble. I collected
a badge and picked up the chalk to write a name—I always
wrote a different name. Today I was Anne.

I entered the back room where sick pets were in cages and
began cleaning them. Many people started this job, thinking
it would be fun because they'd see cute animals; then they
saw the cages full of sick and recovering pets and recoiled
from cleaning them. The first time the vet and owner, Jason,
showed me the cages, I didn't flinch. When he told me most
people did, I laughed. "They probably didn't live in a refugee
camp for years."

We used communal toilets when we lived in a refugee camp at an airport in Tuzla. During a downpour, the portable toilets flooded, and sewerage and mud mingled between the white tents. Every day for a week, we had to tramp through the faeces and live with the smell. After that, nothing much shook me.

I checked the chart attached to the cage in which a lethargic tabby lay, his back shaved where they had performed surgery to remove a tumour. When I opened the cage, the tabby rubbed against my hand for cuddles. "You're feeling better, Roscoe." He purred gently.

I cleaned out the cage, refreshing his water. Roscoe plonked on my lap, and I gently patted him before transferring him back to the cage. After cleaning all the cages, I went to the back room where we kept those that had to quarantine.

In a cage was a Rottweiler puppy suffering from the deadly Parvovirus. The cage smelled of the diarrhoea and vomit that the puppy had expelled; he was on an IV drip and was lying listlessly in his cage. When I opened the door, his glassy eyes didn't follow me. He was on his way out. I had seen the death stare many times.

I gently placed the puppy on a blanket and took the cage outside the back door. I would need to clean and disinfect it before it could be used again. I returned with a warm cloth and a bucket of warm water. I sat on the floor and placed the puppy on my lap, gently washing him. "It's okay, my little buddy. You're going to a better place." I remained with him, even though I heard the bell dinging at the front as customers lined up.

Jason came to the door. "Seka, there's a line."

"They can wait." I gently stroked the puppy. We had injections to help put animals to sleep, but this required time and consent. Jason had noted on the chart that he'd called the owners three times this morning and hadn't received a call back. I wouldn't let any living creature die alone, without the connection of human touch, one glimmer of what this world could be. "He doesn't have long."

Jason nodded and returned to the front desk. He understood the randomness of life. His parents had survived the Khmer Rouge in Cambodia. His father was in a labour camp and survived starvation, boiling a leather belt as sustenance.

This puppy didn't have a chance. The wrong family adopted him as a birthday present for their five-year-old. The idiots didn't want to pay for a vaccination and only brought him to the vet for treatment because their son was screaming for his puppy. The puppy's lungs fluttered as he struggled to breathe. It was the death rattle. I cradled him tightly against me as he expired. "There, you're better now."

I removed the IV drip that was sedating him from pain and picked him up, taking him to the room where we kept the remains. Wealthy owners cremated their beloved pets and returned them to the family, or they could have them cremated and buried in a pet cemetery. I doubted that would be the pup's fate. I wrapped the pup in the disposal bag and placed his remains in the freezer.

Jason came in as I was washing my hands. "You'll have to call the owner and ask them if they want to collect his remains and bury him," I told him. Owners who neglected to vaccinate their pets would not shell out for cremation. A council worker would collect and dispose of the pup in a landfill. "And tell the fuckers to vaccinate any other puppies." The owners would probably do a swap and switch—get another puppy and pretend it was all better to save their son from having a shitty memory of his birthday.

The shit people did to sanitise death from their life perplexed me. Only those privileged by geography in capitalist societies had that choice—they believed they would live forever, believed that they were special, believed they were above the scourge of illness and death. I'd learned since I was 15 years old that death was our shadow, and we were living on borrowed time. The only question was when and how.

I went to the counter and checked in new patients.

Sitting in the kitchen reading a vet magazine during morning tea, I heard Ninu talking to Jason in reception. I hadn't spoken to Ninu since our aborted date. I eyed the back door, thinking about ducking out and hiding. The only thing that stayed me was that I would have to see him eventually. May as well get it over and done with.

"What are your plans this weekend?" Jason asked.

"Pig hunting with the cousins," I heard Ninu's deep voice reply.

"Where?"

"In the scrub around Kyneton. They're wild, and my cousin has a smokehouse. He makes his own bacon from the pigs. You?"

"I have a race this weekend. Have to hold my record." Jason rode his bike to work every day, a 70 km round trip, and competed in bike races nearly every weekend. They exchanged small talk for a few minutes.

"I'm here for the kelpie," Ninu said.

"Go through the back. Seka will get her for you," Jason said.

I stood as Ninu came in. His brown eyes looked at me and quickly away. "Jason said you'd get the kelpie."

He would not make this easy on me. "Can we go out the back and talk?"

Ninu nodded and went ahead of me to the back of the clinic. "You don't need to say anything," he cut me off. "I know you don't feel the same way, and this is over. You didn't need to run away on our date though."

"That's not why I ran." I closed the door behind me. "Do you remember when I told you I survived Srebrenica and the siege?"

Ninu nodded.

"I saw one of the Serb War Criminals who tormented us that night. I followed him home."

"That's horrible." He approached, placing his hands on my shoulders. "Are you okay?"

"I'm fine." I recapped my conversation with Alyssa. "I hope they indict and arrest him. It's just a matter of time."

"I'm so sorry you had to go through that." Ninu hugged me.

I knew I should detach, not let him get the wrong idea. My muscles relaxed, and I sagged against him with relief, my head tucking under his chin, his arms holding me tight. It was so nice to have someone strong to lean against. I had to carry the burden of Silver Cross alone.

"I'm sorry I didn't call you," I murmured against his chest. "My head has just been all over the place."

"So you wanted to call me?" Ninu lifted my face.

His eyelashes were so thick that it looked like he had eyeliner around his bottom lids. They were full of desire and warmth as they looked at me. I wanted to sink into him and forget my life for a little while.

"Yes, I did," I murmured.

He bent and kissed me. I put my hands through his hair, breathing in his aftershave as desire warmed my blood. We pulled apart, and I quickly straightened my work shirt.

"Do you want to go out on Saturday?" he asked.

"Yes." I smiled.

We arranged for him to pick me up a few blocks from my house in front of a park. My mother and brother would be scandalised because I was dating a non-Muslim, so he couldn't come to my door.

We entered the clinic, and I went to the back and found the kelpie. "What a good girl you are!" I gently stroked her silky fur. The dog was completely happy, tail wagging. My heart clutched as I handed her over to Ninu. *Please let her owners find her in time.* Last week, he'd picked up a Burmese cat. I didn't ask if her owners had reunited with her. It was better not to know whether she'd been euthanised.

"See you Saturday," Ninu said as he walked out, a jaunt in his step.

I felt pretty jaunty myself as I worked my shift.

Before the end of my shift, I checked my emails, butterflies in my stomach when I saw Alyssa's email address.

Dear Seka

Good news. The War Tribunal has appointed a lawyer to collect your testimony. I have booked a meeting room at our offices. Are you available this Friday at 3 pm?

Regards

Alyssa

Alyssa then provided the address.

I re-read the email, a sense of unreality descending. It was really happening. We would bring Silver Cross to justice. On Friday, I had my tutorial at university. I would have to leave early and miss the second half to make my appointment with Alyssa. A small sacrifice to pay.

I breathed in and out, calming myself, as my trembling fingers formed a reply, confirming my attendance at the meeting.

I looked at the clock and saw it was 5 o'clock. I turned off the computer and went to the door, Jason locking up behind me. He had changed out of his work gear and was wearing his lycra biking outfit.

"See you tomorrow," he said as he jumped on his bike.

I waved and walked towards the train station, bypassing the platform for the train line home, instead of catching the Epping train that stopped at Thornbury. When I got off the train, I walked down Clarendon Street and past Silver Cross' house. A lush gum tree stood proudly in his front yard, its emerald leaves swaying gently in the breeze, framing the picturesque weatherboard house. It was a balmy summer evening, and the curtains to his living room window fluttered in the breeze. The bright light from his house framed him in the window as he sat at the dining table, eating dinner alone in his bus driver shirt. The television was on, and he was watching *The Price is Right*. Silver Cross got up and disappeared from view, returning with a beer in hand. While he was gone, the German Shepherd leapt up, his two front paws on the dining table, and licked the plate, taking off a piece of meat.

"Damn it, Lux," Silver Cross shouted, yanking the dog by the leash. They disappeared from view, and the front door opened. Silver Cross pushed the dog out and closed the door. He returned to the dining table, took the plate back to the kitchen and returned with another serving. The dog leapt up to the front window, whining at his owner.

Silver Cross got up and closed the curtains. The dog sat staring at the window plaintively. I walked up the block and crossed the street so I could walk down in front of Silver Cross' house. The dog was still with his back to the street, staring at the window, waiting for his owner to come and get him.

I rifled through my handbag and took out the dried pig trotters I'd taken from the vets. As I approached the mesh fence, I waved it against the fence. Lux's ears straightened up like an antenna, and he trotted towards me, his pink tongue lolling out of his mouth.

"Hello, Lux," I murmured. His brown eyes met mine, flickering with recognition at the sound of his name. "Here you go, boy." I slipped the pig trotters through the gaps in the fence. Lux took them gently, his jaws closing around the treat with careful precision. "Good boy." I reached over, brushing my fingers over the soft fur on his head. He leaned into my touch, but I didn't linger. As I walked on, I glanced back. Lux had already returned to the front door, sprawled on his belly, contentedly gnawing his treat. We were firm friends now.

On Friday, I walked to the foyer of the high-rise where The Argus offices were. Alyssa greeted me in front of the elevator.

"How are you?" she asked, kissing me on the cheek.

I wore jeans and a black jacket, the closest I came to formal wear. I didn't want to oversell the professional look.

"Nervous," I said.

Alyssa nodded. She led me to a meeting room. Waiting inside was a blonde woman, a short blonde bob perfectly coiffed, tasteful pink lipstick and a light dusting of foundation, a black power suit.

"I'm Luna Bernard." The blonde offered her hand, gave me a firm handshake. "I'm here representing the War Tribunal and to collect your testimony."

"Seka Torlak." I shook hands with her, introducing myself.

We sat at the table across from each other. Alyssa sat on my side, a few seats up. She was taking notes for the article, but wouldn't report anything until the arrest.

"I've looked over your notes, and I'm here to take your official testimony. You said you saw the accused, Miroslav Vlahović, at Potočari Industrial Complex on the night of 11 July 1995. Please give me your testimony about what you experienced that night?"

Hearing Silver Cross name coming from her mouth threw me for a moment. How could this inhuman criminal have a name?

"Ms Torlak?" Luna prompted when I didn't speak.

I took a deep, shaky breath.

"Yes, I saw him on that night. We had arrived that morning. The town was being overtaken by the Serbs, and we thought we would be safe at the UN base because the Serbs wouldn't attack us that close."

I was back in Srebrenica, running down the narrow road with thousands of other residents toward Potočari. Bosnian soldiers urged us to return home, assuring us they would defend the town, but three years of starvation and deprivation had made us too afraid.

When we left our house, my father told Mama not to lock the front door in case there was looting. So we left it unlocked, with food still cooking on the stove, thinking we would return to eat.

"My father and brother went to the forest and hid there. Because they were both soldiers, the enemy would have captured them and shot them."

I remembered my last glimpse of my father as he and Emir walked away from us. Mortar shells were exploding on the road, sending debris and body parts around us. There were shrieks of pain and fear as we ducked and weaved, hoping to be lucky enough to dodge another shell.

"When we arrived at the base, there were thousands and thousands of refugees around. The UN wouldn't let any of us enter behind the mesh fence, so we spread out into the factories, seeking shelter."

The smell of sweat and fear filled my nostrils once again.

"The UN soldiers were dancing and singing. They were happy that the town fell because they would now go home."

Even though intellectually I knew that the Dutchbat contingent was hopelessly outnumbered and in no position to fight the Serbs, they shouldn't have rejoiced in our surrender. They were complicit in the death of those taken.

"During the first night, packs of Serbs walked around the factory, searching for jewellery and money to steal. A group approached us, using a torch to examine us for gold. They saw my necklace." I touched the silver coin around my neck and lifted it up. "They thought it might be valuable. Silver Cross, I mean, Miroslav." I nearly gagged just saying his name. "He examined the necklace, turning it over in his fingers, then scoffed when he realised it was only silver—worthless to him. He called me a real patriot and said I should keep it, a token of my 'silver town.'" Mocking Srebrenica which was named for its silver. I tucked the necklace back under my top, its weight pressing against my skin like a memory I couldn't shake.

"A Serb next to him used the torch to view my body. He wanted to take me with them, but then they saw the blood on my thighs. I'd gotten my period, and the t-shirt strips Mama used to stem it were overflowing. It was what saved me from being taken away." I took a sip of water, my hand shaking. "They took another young girl next to us. She returned hours later with blood flowing down her thighs. She hung herself from the factory walkway during the night."

"How are you sure that Miroslav Vlahović is the man you call Silver Cross?" Luna asked.

"I recognised his face from the night. He has different hair, it's cut short now. He has a silver tooth on his left incisor, and that's how I knew it was definitely him. The tooth glinted in the torchlight."

Alyssa jotted notes in her notebook, watching us.

"Thank you very much for your testimony," Luna said, packing her papers in her suitcase. "We will see if we can verify your testimony with other witnesses from the night before and investigate Miroslav Vlahović."

"How long until he's arrested?" I demanded.

"This is just the preliminary stage," Luna said. "We will collect further corroborating testimony, and when we have enough evidence, we will indict him and seek an arrest warrant for Australia."

After the lawyer left, I turned to Alyssa. "How do you think that went?"

"Good. It was great you had so much information about him that they could investigate. And I've already started collecting information about Miroslav."

"What do you have?"

Alyssa hesitated before opening her notebook. "Miroslav arrived in Australia on the 1st September 1995, with his wife and two daughters on a refugee visa. He was originally a resident of Medeno Polje and became a refugee when the Bosnian army claimed it as part of the free territory. In 1996, he qualified for his bus driver's licence in Australia and has worked as a bus driver since." Alyssa closed her notebook.

"I'm hoping to infiltrate the Serb community by approaching a community centre to interview Serb refugees and find out more about him. I have to be careful, though, not to spook him and make him feel targeted. But if I can confirm his war service record, that would be one step closer to verifying that he is Silver Cross."

"How long do you think it will take for him to be indicted?" I asked.

"I'm not going to lie to you, Seka, we're in this for the long haul. But I promise you I will do everything I can to write an air-tight article about him and expose him as a war criminal. This will pressure the government to issue an indictment and get the wheels of justice moving." Alyssa walked me to the elevator. "We are getting there. We just have to collect evidence, and you have to be patient."

It was well and good for the lawyer and journalist to encourage patience, but I'd been waiting for four years. Four years with no justice in sight. How much more would I have to wait?

"You know it was a fluke that I saw him that day in the city. If I had been just a few seconds later, I would have missed him entirely. Yet I did, I saw him."

"I know, and it's because of your initial investigation that we've come so far. Now it's up to me to finish this."

The elevator arrived, and I entered. As it closed and I descended to the foyer, I kept hearing Alyssa's voice about infiltrating the Serb community. The best person to infiltrate the Serb community would be a Serb. I knew what I had to do. Alyssa was wrong. It was up to me.

6-Stalker

I left a note for my mother telling her I was going to the uni library to study and took my backpack of textbooks when I left the house on Sunday morning. During the 30-minute train trip to Flinders Street Station, I caught up on my weekly reading for the subject Animal Diversity, highlighting and annotating my bound reader of photocopied articles the lecturer had selected. As I transferred to the Cranbourne train, I began working on an Introduction to Animal Diversity essay, making notes about the different classifications. In the one and a half hours it took me to arrive at Cranbourne train station, I had drafted half my essay in my notebook, listing footnotes to the quotes I would use from my reader.

I stepped onto the platform, my pulse quickening. It had been nearly six months since I last made this journey. With my hood pulled low and sunglasses shielding my eyes, I walked down High Street, keeping my head down. At Clarendon Street, I turned right, my steps measured, my breath steady. Halfway up the street, I reached it—the white weatherboard house with its green-tiled roof and matching awnings, unchanged yet weighted with memory. I didn't go closer. Instead, I leaned against the weeping willow across the street, its branches swaying like silent sentinels.

It was mid-morning, and the curtains were open. The front door opened, and the family trooped out. Zora's parents were greyer and more rotund since their days in Srebrenica. Her father, Slobodan, was a miner in Srebrenica. I wondered what he did in Australia. There weren't any mines in Victoria. I assumed he probably worked in a factory where he needed little English or any particular skills to undertake the assembly line. Her mother's hair was grey and cut short. She was a stay-at-home mother, always occupied with caring for her five children. Only three children walked with them—Zora's two younger sisters, now adolescents, and Zora herself, trailing at the back. Her thin, lithe frame was wrapped in a floral dress, her blonde hair cut into a short bob that framed her face. I hadn't seen her two older brothers in a while. Had they married? Started families of their own? The thought lingered as I followed the family down the winding backstreets. I stayed in their wake for five minutes until they reached the community hall—a space the congregation rented for the Serbian Orthodox Church.

When we first arrived in Australia, I'd caught the Cranbourne train, wanting desperately to see Zora. I'd carried the letter she wrote and passed on through Alyssa in my pocket for years, imagining the day we would see each other.

We had gone through so much together. We grew up side by side. Our fathers were best friends, our families intertwined as if we were related. We hadn't distinguished between the religious holidays: her family came to our house for Ramadan; we went to her family for Orthodox Easter and Christmas, and we celebrated Communist Days like the birthday of Tito on 7 May every year. I hadn't known that she was any different from me. Even though I was Muslim and she was Orthodox, religion had played no part in our friendship. It was only when the war started that we were suddenly so different.

When Serbs attacked Srebrenica, I had to live in the woods with my family while the Bosnian army scrambled and eventually expelled them. While we were gone, Zora's family hid our white-goods and sentimental belongings so they weren't looted and destroyed. Upon our return, most Serb residents had abandoned the town, but Zora's father didn't consider himself a nationalist and refused to leave his home. The Serbs who besieged us considered them traitors, and Zora's family home was shelled to the ground. The Muslim refugees who were ethnically cleansed from their villages also saw Zora and her family as Serb enemies and attacked them. Ultimately, they were forced to escape Srebrenica and made their way to Australia.

We had planned our whole lives together when we were young. I chose to go to the veterinarian high school, and then we were supposed to go to university together. When we graduated, we would open a practice together called A New Dawn, inspired by Zora's first name, which meant dawn in English. Now, when I think back to it, it was always Zora's dream to be a vet, but somewhere along the way, I got swept up in the wave, and it became my dream too.

When we came to Australia, I wondered about whether it was the right path when I completed my high school certificate in adult classes. Perhaps there was something else I might want to do, but my mother and Emir had sacrificed so much.

They dedicated themselves to helping me achieve my dream, so I studied veterinary science.

Was Zora still achieving her dream? I had wondered if I would see her at my university until I realised that even if she went to university, she would go to Deakin, which was on this side of the city, so our paths would never cross. I attempted to come during the week a few times, hoping to follow her, see where her day-to-day was, but whenever I tried, the house was abandoned, or I caught glimpses of family members returning home by car or public transport, but there were never any clues that would answer my questions.

She had a head start because she and her family left Srebrenica in 1992, four years before us, and would have arrived in Australia soon after. She had the opportunity to be an Australian high school student, to begin university as a regular student and be the same age as her peers. While I wasn't the only mature age student in my class, I still felt like the odd one out. I was three years older than the regular students, and most of the other mature age students were older than me. I gravitated toward the older mature age students who had more life experience, while I desperately wanted to be friends with the young ones, but whenever I tried, they seemed so vapid and silly. They didn't know who they were, what they wanted, who they liked. They were like wisps in the wind, disintegrating and reforming. Zora and I had supported each other, challenged each other as we competed. Now I had no one to compete with, no one to whom the minutia of everyday study mattered, and so, even though I excelled at all my classes and collected High Distinctions like confetti, there was still a constant hollowness inside. An emptiness that wouldn't be filled.

Before Zora left Srebrenica, we'd promised to find each other, and when I first travelled on the train, I was sure that when I reached her house, I would knock on the door, go to see her and hug her. That her father, Slobodan, and I would weep together as I told him about losing my father, that her mother, Petra, would want to know how my mother was coping. But when I saw their house, I hesitated, unsure about my reception and whether I would see the Zora I knew and loved, or see her as an extension of an enemy. It was a Sunday like this one, and I had followed the family from their house to the church. After they went in, I stood under the open windows on a warm summer day. I listened to the sermon the priest was preaching about how Bosnian Muslims were the ones responsible for the war. About how we were liars, inventing massacres that never happened.

I listened and cried. I tore Zora's letter and left it on the ground, determined to forget I ever knew her. But still, I made the pilgrimage every few months to watch Zora and her family walk to church. I knew it was masochistic to put myself in the path of pain, but I wanted a glimpse of my former life. As I followed them, I was terrified they would recognise me, yet some part of me wanted them to see me, imagining the confrontation.

I knew it was hypocritical to be angry at them for going to church. After all, I attended the mosque too. Since the breakup of what was Yugoslavia and the war, everyone sought a sense of community, and religious traditions gave communities a sense of belonging and identity. Our Imam had also delivered his share of sermons about maintaining cultural purity and how we were the persecuted race, and there was so much anti-Serb sentiment proliferating at the mosque. It didn't mean that Zora and her family were also genocide deniers. Maybe they, too, needed a sense of community and belonging. But no matter how much I rationalised, I couldn't cross the street. I was too scared of confirming my fears and destroying the last few remnants of hope that I had.

Usually, these forays would leave me emotionally battered as I tore myself apart debating about what I should do, but today I was a woman on a mission. I wasn't here to reconnect. I was here to conduct some reconnaissance to put my plan into action.

Zora's hair was shoulder-length, a neat bob parted on the side. When we were children, her mother cut it short, exasperated by having so many young children and in no mood to brush Zora's long hair. Zora was tall and lithe. She had always been slightly taller than me, and now her limbs were long and lean beneath her sleeveless dress. Her skin was so pale, she was translucent, the lines on her skin visible. She had a way of walking with her back straight, her legs elegantly sauntering. Did she always walk like this? The Zora of my childhood was always running. We chased each other up and down the hill to Ćelo, the tree we named and was our secret meeting place where we could hide from our families. It was where she read her mother's romance novels, reading the titillating love scenes out loud and laughing.

I wondered what else had changed? Did she have a boyfriend? Was he a Serb? Would she fulfil the wog dream of intermarrying to propagate the family line? Did she feel trapped, like I did, between her family's expectations and who she really wanted to be? Probably not. She'd had more time to acclimate to Australia. To find herself. She was ahead of me in every way.

All I had were questions about what she was doing, so I would merge truth and fiction to create a new Zora. It would not be a perfect impersonation, but she was the only person I knew well enough whose skin I could wear.

My mission completed, I strode into the train station. I still had a few errands to complete today to implement my plan.

Two and a half hours later, I stepped off the train at Thornbury station and sprinted to Psarakos to buy supplies before walking past Silver Cross' house. Lux barked as I passed. I fed him a treat I'd bought at Psarakos, quickly tossing it through the fence. I walked around the block and back. Lux whined when I passed. I threw another treat. After my third trek, I put on sunglasses and took out the clipboard and pen I'd bought. I knocked on the door of a house two doors up, pretending to be an activist collecting signatures against the redevelopment of a former convent into housing apartments, an issue I had noted in the Serbian newspaper I'd read weeks ago. The resident signed begrudgingly and sent me on my way. I knocked on the door of the next house. The homeowner opened the door and promptly closed it in my face. I entered Silver Cross's front yard and rang his doorbell, my fingers clenched around the pen. My plan hinged on him not being home. The doorbell echoed in the silent house. As I stepped down the front porch, I quickly opened the side gate and hurried down the front path. Holding a pet treat in my hand, Lux trotted behind me.

When we'd reached the end of the street, I clipped on the dog collar I'd bought.

We walked a few streets down, the German Shepherd loping beside me, before I returned to the main road and the next train station. Half an hour later, I was back in Sunshine and at the vet clinic where I worked.

"You're not on," Keisha said as I walked in.

"Yeah, I found this wanderer. Thought I'd check where he lived and get him home."

I went to the back and found the scanner, placing it against Lux's neck while he tried to lick me. The microchip showed the owner's phone number. I lifted the phone and dialled the number, placing my hand on the cradle and hanging up. I pretended to leave a message, giving the name of the vet clinic and phone number.

"His owners will be in tomorrow," I lied to Keisha as I placed Lux in a cage. I provided him with dry food and water. "You'll be safe here tonight." I gave him a pat before I left for the night.

I hopped back on the train and went to Phuong-Vy's bungalow. She wasn't home, so I sat on her front steps, drifting to sleep as I leaned against her front door.

"Seka, what are you doing here?" Phuong-Vy shook me awake.

I rubbed my eyes. Next to her was Tom, wearing his signature white singlet and baggy jeans, holding boxes of produce.

"I needed your help." I rifled through my backpack and took out the peroxide and dye I'd bought. "Ninu invited me to a costume party and I want to go as Marilyn Monroe."

Phuong-Vy clapped her hands in delight. "A makeover. Yes. But you don't have to dye your hair. You can just wear a blonde wig." She unlocked her front door, taking in the plastic bags she'd put down. I followed her in, Tom behind me. Tom placed the produce box on the kitchen table while Phuong-Vy went to a cupboard and returned with a short blonde wig.

"I know, but I want a makeover. I want a new look to mark the beginning of my new life."

Phuong-Vy made eye contact. "Yes, I know what you mean."

"Can you do it now?" I asked.

"Now." She returned the wig to the cupboard. "I had plans. We were going to hang out." She looked at Tom and smiled.

"Oh," I made my lip tremble.

"It's okay babe. I've got some errands to run and I'll be back later," Tom said, glancing at his phone.

Phuong-Vy walked him out, and I heard them murmuring by the front door before she returned, her cheeks pink and mouth swollen.

Phuong-Vy sat me on a kitchen chair as she prepared the dye and foils.

"How's it going with Tom?" I asked.

"Great. We've been seeing each other a few times a week. Today we went to Footscray market and I'm going to make dumplings for dinner."

"Yum." My mouth watered. Phuong-Vy's dumplings were to die for.

"He's so charming and fun. So respectful…" She used a brush to paint the peroxide on my hair and then wrap the strands in foils.

"But," I prompted, noticing the way her voice dropped off.

"I haven't actually ever gone to his place. He says his room-mate is a pig and doesn't want me to see how revolting it is."

"Well then, he doesn't know you," I said, snorting with laughter. Like me, Phuong-Vy had a cast-iron stomach and nothing revolted her. We'd once ended up at a party hosted by my ex where he and his mates did heroin and shat their pants, which then set off the other half who vomited. Phuong-Vy and I laughed like loons as we stepped around the bodily fluids. Phuong-Vy laughed too.

"Sounds like you've got some doubts about him," I said.

She sighed. "I wonder if I'm overthinking it. I mean, he doesn't push for any intimacy and respects what I want."

"But now you're wondering if he's so respectful because he's got someone else to satisfy his needs."

"Hmmm," she sighed.

"The best way to deal with it is to insist. You've got to get pushy."

"I know." She squeezed my shoulder.

We watched video hits she'd taped on her VCR while we waited for the dye to take. After she'd washed it out in the kitchen sink, she layered my hair into a short bob. Tom arrived as she was blow-drying it.

"How does she look?" Phuong-Vy asked.

"Stunning." Tom stared at me a touch too long.

"Thanks," I muttered under my breath as I viewed myself in a hand-held mirror. "Can I borrow your blue contact lenses?" I asked.

Phuong-Vy brought them out and showed me how to put them in. My eyes were watering by the time I placed them in my eyes. I looked in the mirror in amazement at my transformation. I looked like Zora.

"Thank you, thank you." I hugged Phuong-Vy, feeling happy and light. My plan was going to succeed. "I'll get them back to you in a few days." I took out the contact lenses, and Phuong-Vy showed me how to disinfect them.

I packed up the contact lens cleaner. "I'd better get out of your hair."

"You can stay. We were just going to have a few drinks." Tom held up the paper bag he'd brought and took out the vodka.

"No, I have to get home or my Mum will kill me."

I sprinted home. I had a busy day tomorrow.

7-Ruse

I woke up feeling heavy, my head throbbing from a night of restless tossing and turning, my mind tangled in the fantasies of my ruse finally playing out. Dragging myself out of bed, I stepped into the hallway on my way to the bathroom—only to find Mama standing there. The moment her eyes landed on me, she screamed. I jolted, my pulse spiking.

"*Bože Sačuvaj*," God save us, she exclaimed as she looked at me with shock.

"What?" I asked.

"What did you do to your hair?" she demanded, reaching over and touching it.

I saw the blonde strands before my face and realised what had felt different. "Oh, I wanted a new look." I smoothed my hands through the short bob. "Do you like it?"

"Tsk, tsk." Mama shook her head.

Emir appeared in the hallway, holding toast in his hand.

"Look what your sister did?" Mama pointed at my head.

"You're just like every wog girl trying to be Anglo." He shrugged and returned to the kitchen.

"I like it." I stepped into the bathroom and shut the door firmly behind me. Facing the mirror, I studied my reflection, startled by the unfamiliarity of my own face. My skin looked paler, almost ghostly. Phuong-Vy had lightened my eyebrows, making my brown eyes seem lighter. I looked like a washed-out, faded version of myself. She had warned me—I'd need makeup to make the hair work. Now, I understood why.

After showering and brushing my teeth, I returned to my bedroom and slipped into my jeans and black t-shirt. As I blow-dried my hair, I caught glimpses of my reflection, still adjusting to the change. I tucked the contact lenses and make-up bag into my backpack. Mama couldn't see me wearing either. After a quick breakfast, I headed out the door, a spring in my step. Today was the day.

When I walked into work, Keisha looked up at the door. "Can I help you?" she asked as I walked on. She peered closer, gaping. "Is that you Seka?"

I smiled. "Yeah, a new look for a costume party tonight. What do you think?"

"Wow, you're almost unrecognisable. Are you wearing contacts?"

I nodded. I'd gone to the McDonald's and put on makeup using Phuong-Vy's foundation, which was ivory and made me look paler, highlighting my fake blue eyes with blue eyeliner and eyeshadow, pink lipstick and a faint rosiness of blush to accentuate my cheeks.

"Has the German Shepherd been picked up?" I asked.

Keisha shook his head.

"I'll call them again." After I put my work gear in my locker, I got my name tag and wrote the name Zora on it, feeling a thrill as I shaped the letters.

I called the phone number on the microchip tag I'd memorised, my stomach fluttering as I squeezed the handset on the phone tightly. *Please pick up*, I chanted in my head.

"Hello," his voice answered.

"Good morning," I said, deliberately making my voice cheerful. "Can I speak to Miroslav Vlahović?" I pronounced his name correctly, emphasising the 'ich' in the suffix. I held my breath as I waited.

"That's me."

"Mr Vlahović, my name is Zora Đokić and I'm calling from Sunshine Veterinary clinic. We have a German Shepherd named Lux, who belongs to you here."

"He's okay? He's safe?" Miroslav asked, his voice choked up.

"Yes, he's perfectly healthy. A resident found him wandering near the train station and brought him to us."

"Where is Sunshine?" Miroslav asked. "How did he get there?"

"We're in the western suburbs," I said. "Around twelve kilometres from the city."

"That's on the other side of the city. I'm in Thornbury."

"Well, sometimes some people steal dogs from yards. Either they reconsidered, or Lux escaped." I'd already had time to prepare for this scenario. "Do you have a pen and paper so I can give you the address?"

"Yes, yes, of course."

I heard him rifling around, and then he returned on the line. I dictated the address and told him about using the council offices as a landmark.

"I'll be there in an hour," Miroslav said.

"Wonderful." I did a fist wave. "We'll see you soon then."

I hung up and did a little dance.

"Someone's happy?" Keisha asked as she entered the stockroom and took a bag of pet food.

"The owner of the German Shepherd is coming in to get his pet."

"Yay." Keisha lifted her hand in a high five. We didn't get many good news stories, so it was always a big hurrah when we did.

"But why did you use that name?" she asked, nodding toward the name badge with Zora on it.

"He's Serb and I don't know if he's one of those people who's going to be all weird about talking to a Bosnian, so I'm using a Serb name."

"Honestly, some people need to let bygones be bygones. All that shit happened overseas. You're all Australians now."

"I agree, but you know how it is."

We'd had an incident a few months ago where a Serb woman refused to allow me to check her in when she heard my name and found out I was Bosnian-Muslim.

I saw him step out of the blue Toyota Camry through the clinic window. He walked differently than when I'd last seen him at Potočari. There he had moved with the limberness of a wolf on the hunt. Now he was just another middle-aged man.

Thankfully, I was the only one on reception with Keisha taking her break, and I smiled encouragingly as he walked toward me.

"I'm Miroslav. I'm here for Lux."

"Of course." I smiled wider, imitating relief. "I'm so glad we can reunite you. Let me get him."

As soon as I stepped into the backroom, my knees wobbled slightly, and I had to grab the counter. I hadn't realised putting on such a facade would be such an emotional toll. Anger and rage were coursing through my bloodstream, and I wanted to claw his eyes out. Instead, I had to project calm and serenity. I took a deep breath and pushed my hair away from my face. "You are Zora," I muttered to myself.

I fetched Lux and walked back to the reception area. When he saw him, Lux lunged at his owner, placing his two front paws on Miroslav's chest and licking his face. Miroslav hugged him, closing his eyes as he burrowed his face into the dog's neck. I stood uncomfortably to the side, trying to remember what I usually did in these situations.

"Look how much he missed you," I said, remembering to jump into small talk to ease the awkwardness. Lux jumped down, and I rubbed his back. "You're such a good boy."

Miroslav quickly wiped his eyes. "It's so stupid to love an animal so much." His voice was thick with emotion.

"No, it's only natural. They become a part of our families."

"Zora." He switched to our language. "Are you from the mother country?"

I nodded. "Yes, from Srebrenica. You?" I asked, reverting to our custom of using the royal version of 'we' to signify respect.

"I'm from Medeno Polje. We're twenty kilometres from Srebrenica."

"We're neighbours," I said, feeling dazed. I'd assumed that he was a weekend Četnik, one of the Serbs who came from Serbia to fight on the weekends, viewing it like a game as they played soldiers while we fought for our lives and homes.

"When did you arrive in Australia?" he asked.

"1992." I had to concentrate on not tripping myself up and telling him my arrival date, instead of Zora's. "What about you?"

"1996," he told me what I already knew. "We were chased out of our village early in the war and had to move to the mother country. I joined the Serb army, but there was no life there after the war. We came to Australia."

Well, I was half right. He became a weekend Četnik.

"With your family?" I asked as Lux rubbed himself on my legs. He could probably feel my internal agitation. I reached my hand out and petted his head, calming myself.

"Yes, my wife and two daughters. And you?"

"Oh, my parents and siblings." I looked down into Lux's eyes. His loving gaze centred on me as I lied to the man who killed my Ramo. "I work here as a receptionist while studying to be a veterinarian."

"I was a bus driver overseas, and I'm a bus driver here," Miroslav said.

"Wow, I catch buses all the time. Which route do you drive?" I tensed, wondering if I was being too obvious.

"The number 82. From Moonee Ponds to Footscray."

"That's so great." I smiled with exhilaration and relief. This was exactly what I needed.

The door opened behind him, and a man walked in with a Beagle beside him.

"Well, I'd better leave you to work," Miroslav said, putting on Lux's leash.

"Of course. Ciao Miroslav. Ciao Lux," I said as they walked out.

I watched them walk to the car, where Miroslav opened the passenger door for Lux to sit in. Miroslav patted him as he rolled down the window with his other hand, before closing the door and walking to the driver's seat. Miroslav was a man who loved his dog. There was a way for me to exploit this. As I served my next customer, my brain churned through ideas.

Every day, I had to fight the urge to hop on a train to Thornbury and spy on Miroslav. The plan was in motion—now, it was just a matter of time, of carefully setting each piece into place. I tried to focus on the day-to-day, but it felt like I was sleepwalking through classes and work, my mind elsewhere. My fingers constantly itched to refresh my emails, waiting for an update from Alyssa.

I'd thought about emailing her what I'd learned about Miroslav, but then she'd know what I was up to. No, I had to play the long game, collect as much information as I could about him, and then share it with Alyssa.

I needed a disguise to follow him on the bus undetected and figure out his bus route. With my blonde hair, I was now prominent and imminently recognisable. I locked myself in my bedroom and tried on different disguises. I put on my brother's loose tracksuit pants and cap, attempting to imitate a boy. My curves were too prominent. I attempted flattening my chest with bandages; it felt uncomfortable. I looked too short and slight to be a boy. Knowing my luck, some asshole wogs would try to test their strength against me and bash me.

I put on my mother's skirt and shirt, layering tea towels around my torso to make myself look thick, but I didn't know what to do about my face and hair. I attempted my mother's scarf, which made me look a little more unrecognisable.

I returned to her wardrobe and pulled out the abaya she had bought for prayers at the mosque, along with the matching hijab. Both were black, plain, and unremarkable—perfect. Slipping the hijab over my head, I watched my blonde hair disappear beneath the fabric. The border jutted slightly over my forehead, casting a shadow over my face—the abaya draped loosely, concealing my entire body. I put on a pair of sunglasses and glanced at my reflection. I barely recognised myself. My disguise was complete.

It was a Tuesday, my day off from uni and school, and I left the house with the abaya and hijab in my backpack and changed in the toilets at Footscray train station. I put on my sunglasses and exited the train, walking to Droop Street, where I would get on the bus that Miroslav was supposed to be driving.

I noticed the stares as I walked. Women wrinkled their noses, men stared with dislike.

"Go back where you came from," a young man shouted at me as I passed by the pub.

I caught sight of myself in the window reflection. The hijab and abaya made me look unrecognisable, but they also brought a lot of attention. It was too late now. I had to continue. I hadn't understood the racism and discrimination that Muslim women were subjected to.

I waited at the bus stop and caught people staring at me. Only one woman, an elderly Greek woman wearing a black skirt, shirt, and a headscarf, smiled at me. I wondered what it was that distinguished the two of us. She was covered up as much as I was, but somehow I was subjected to vitriol.

I stepped up on the bus and tripped. The woman behind me had stepped on my abaya, tugging it from around me and making me fall backwards.

"Serves you right, you crow," she swore when I looked at her. She was brown-haired and round like a barrel.

"Fuck you, cunt," I muttered and elbowed her.

Her face turned red with rage, and she formed a fist.

"Stop it, both of you," the Greek Grandma intervened, helping me up the steps. "Be good girls." She wagged her finger at both of us. Barrel Girl looked like she was going to say something, but her friend yanked her elbow and she simmered down.

The Greek Grandma led me to a seat and had me sit at the window.

"Here you go," she said, sitting next to me. "Ah, those Skippy Kangaroos think this country belongs to them. When we came here in 1954, they didn't know what food was. They had a piece of meat and boiled vegetables. We brought them capsicum, eggplant, olives, feta cheese. They called us the criminals. My husband and his friends were beaten at work, beaten on the street. They would call them Abos because we were dark. Kick him on the street like a dog. And now they attack you. You're the latest arrivals. The Muslims. You wear a piece of cloth on your head, I wear a piece of cloth on my head, but your cloth makes you a terrorist, and mine makes me invisible. This country never changes. It keeps being stolen, and everyone thinks it belongs to them and not the newest ones who arrive. Why can't we just share? Why can't we all just live in peace? But now, always attack, attack. Whoever is the latest to make us the big ones."

I nodded along to her as she spoke. Content to listen, agreeing to what she said. I remembered my English tutor at school pointing out that the way Australians knew who the latest wave of immigrants were was based on who owned the Fish and Chip shops. It used to be the Anglos, then the newly arrived migrants from the 50s and 60s. When Australia ran out of white people, they could import with their 50 pound pom scheme, then suddenly Europeans were desired. At first, they wanted the whitest ones, those from Poland, Lithuania, Latvia, Poland. The ones furthest from the equator, whose skin was pale, and were still promoting their White Australia Policy. The waves of migration to Australia were predicated on the waves of disruption and destruction in the countries of origin. It started with the British sending the unwanted convicts, and has always been the dream of a better life. The melting pot with the expectation of assimilating, giving up culture and language, the way they made the Aboriginal people give up their way of life, and still, they were never accepted. And the same thing happened over and over. It doesn't matter that you have a piece of paper declaring you as Australian, you're never accepted as Australian. You're never Australian because the Aussie that everyone believes in is Anglo, and the rest of us are just needed to break our backs for the benefit of the economy, but never to believe we're worth anything more than labourers.

"You're a good girl. Don't let them break you. You live here and you live well. Those Skippy Kangaroos are jealous. They have everything, and they do nothing. We have nothing, but we do everything."

I smiled at her.

"Me and my Dmetri come here with one suitcase each. We live in one bedroom and work in factory. Now we buy house for each of my three children. My grandchildren live good life. We do well. You do hardworking. You create for your family."

I nodded.

"This is my stop." The Ya-Ya got up and waited for the doors to open. She stepped down the stairs and continued walking on, a shopping bag in one arm.

I looked out the front of the bus. Barrel Girl was busy talking to her friend. Apparently, some guy really wanted to fuck her on the weekend. Lucky her.

Miroslav wasn't driving. He could be on the morning, afternoon or evening. I didn't know when the changeover shift occurred. The buses began at 5 am, so I assumed there was an 8-hour shift from 5 am to 1 pm or so. It was 11 am. I had to figure out his shift and then engineer a conversation. My plan hinged on it.

I got off at Footscray, walked around the shops, and got on the bus later in the afternoon. I spotted him. He was on the afternoon shift. Tomorrow was the day. I looked at the time. Tonight I had a date with Ninu I had to get ready for.

8-Date

I waited on the street self-consciously, my backpack on my shoulder. I wore a green, strappy dress that was fitted around the waist and flowed around my hips. It was one of the dresses we'd received from Bosnians earning their *sevap*, credit for good deeds, by donating to the refugees who arrived. When we first arrived, we'd receive bags of clothes and bedding, some of it not even washed and still reeking from its previous occupants. I had had little occasion to wear the dress. It was too booby and therefore not suitable for Bosnian events. I wore a denim jacket when leaving the house so Mama wouldn't see it. But it seemed apt for my date with Ninu. It showed I was attempting to be pretty, but the fabric was cotton, so it also showed I wasn't a try-hard.

At 7 pm on the dot, Ninu screeched to a halt at the tree in front of me in his beaten red pickup. "Wow, you look gorgeous," he said, peering at me through the open passenger door. He'd slicked his hair down and was wearing a blue plaid shirt and jeans, his tanned forearms leaning on the steering wheel.

I opened the door and sat on the seat beside him, placing my backpack at my feet. "For my sleepover at Phuong-Vy's,"

I said. In my backpack, I'd packed for sleeping overnight at Phuong-Vy's, so my mother didn't know how late I stayed out.

"Oh, great." He rubbed the back of his neck while driving. "You know my folks are visiting my uncle in Mytleford, so I've got the place to myself. If you wanted to, you know, crash."

I nodded, giving myself a moment to think. Until now, we'd fooled around in his truck or a park. We'd never been together in a bed or a proper domestic situation.

"That would be nice." It would be a pleasant novelty to have sex in a bed.

"Great, great." Ninu exhaled with relief. "Because I was thinking we could go back there now and I could make you a steak on the barbie, have a beer, and just have a night in."

"So you already had this planned out," I said.

"No, well, not completely. We can also go out. There's a great pub I know, with great food."

I wrinkled my nose as he spoke. Pubs had never been my scene. I'd tried a few times, but they were places for people who truly enjoyed drinking—something I had never mastered. I'd flirted with alcohol before, especially in Srebrenica, chasing the numbness it promised, trying to forget. But I could never fully let go. So eventually, I just stopped trying.

"Yes, to the steak and no to the beer. I don't drink," I told Ninu. It had become easier just to claim that I was a Muslim for not drinking or being peer pressured to drink by fuckwits who couldn't 'have fun' without binge-drinking.

"You don't. Why?" he asked.

We'd never actually gone on a date, so he'd never had cause to ask. The closest we came to a date was Phuong-Vy's birthday outing, which I'd bailed on.

"Look, I usually tell people it's because I'm Muslim, but that's not it really. I don't believe in much of anything. I just hate the taste and how it makes me feel, and I really hate feeling out of control."

Drinking made me feel paranoid. It relaxed my guard and meant I was vulnerable, a situation that was untenable when you spent your adolescence in the middle of a war zone or in a refugee camp—being unaware of your surroundings and dangers equated to death.

Ninu drove toward the freeway, and then instead of turning onto it, he continued straight up a road bordered by farms on either side. There were signs about strawberry picking and cherries and fruit for sale. Ninu turned left and followed a road. On my left was a valley, and cows grazed the green grass there. Even though we were only 15 minutes from suburbia, it was like we were in the country.

We passed a winemaking farm and a horse farm. Ninu took left and right turns until I couldn't keep track anymore and pulled into a driveway guarded by a metal gate with the sign Micallef's Farm.

"Is that your surname?" I asked, realised that even though we'd been seeing each other casually for the past three months, we were light on the conversation.

He nodded. "Hey, what's your surname?"

"Torlak."

"Seka Torlak," he said, pronouncing my name properly, enunciating the 'r' the way Europeans did.

"Wow, you said that properly."

"I am a Maltese," he said. "My tongue is broken with my mother tongue."

"You can speak Maltese?" I asked.

"Inti sabiħa."

"What did you say?" I asked, my pulse quickening at the intense way he looked at me.

"You are beautiful."

"Sabiha is a name in Bosnian. It must be Arabic." I said, wanting to deflect the sudden charged tension in the truck's cabin.

"The Maltese are a melting pot of cultures. Every nation known to man has conquered and occupied us," Ninu said, taking the hint.

"Oh, wow, thank you." *Shut up Seka.*

Ninu drove down the driveway in front of a long one-storey yellow brick house with a double garage beside it. "Home sweet home." He stopped the car and leaned over to kiss me. I relaxed into his embrace, relieved to find common ground in our physical attraction. Sex I could do, emotion was out.

Ninu came around to my side of the truck. When I got out, he took my backpack and tossed it over his shoulder, taking my hand in his. "This is my parent's house." He nodded to the yellow brick house and walked around the corner and down a side path. In the backyard was a covered patio area with a hot tub, an outside couch with a cane coffee table, and a dining table and chairs. He continued walking through it to a yellow-bricked bungalow at the bottom of the backyard. "This is my crib." He used his keys and unlocked the door.

I followed him inside. It was a two-bedroom unit with a small kitchenette opening into a living room. The walls were white, the furniture monochrome, the couch grey, the small table and chairs black, and the bedhead in the bedroom black iron, but it was immaculately clean.

"It's nice," I said, peering into the second bedroom with a single bed and a desk with a computer.

"Thanks. Dad and I built it together," Ninu said, looking at the walls with pride.

"Wow, that's pretty amazing." I felt myself unexpectedly tearing up. This would have happened to me and my brother Emir if we'd lived in Bosnia. Our father had built a three-storey house and was going to convert the second and third floors into flats for Emir and me to live in. He, too, had planned to work with my brother to create homes for our future. Instead, it all turned to ash, and the house my father built now belonged to strangers who contributed to our extermination.

"Are you okay?" Ninu asked, approaching and placing his arm gently on my shoulder.

"Yes, just having some hay fever. I might have to take my pills." I reached for my backpack and rooted around inside so I could hide my face under my curtain of hair.

"Do you want to call Phuong-Vy and tell her you're staying over?" He nodded to the phone on the kitchen island.

"Great idea." I found my hay fever tablets and took them to the kitchen, popping a blister and taking them with a glass of water. Better safe than sorry.

"I'll get our dinner ready while you call," Ninu said, opening the fridge and removing two steaks and a plate of chopped vegetables. The plate was piled with capsicum, eggplant, mushrooms, and zucchini. "I've also got a potato salad. You bring it out when you've finished." He nodded to a bowl still in the fridge.

I nodded. He gave me a quick peck on the cheek and left through the front door. I watched him through the window as he turned on the barbecue, fiddling with the knobs, and then starting the fire. It was a novelty seeing a man cook. My father had been hands-off in the house with a clear division between women's and men's labour, and my brother was the same. My mother and I were the ones who completed all the domestic chores and prepared meals. The closest my brother came to cooking was making himself a sandwich, and even that was lazily done with a few ingredients clumsily slapped together. I wondered who cleaned Ninu's house? Did he do that too, or was it his mother? I'd have to ask. I didn't want to be impressed by false advertising.

I picked up the phone and dialled Phuong-Vy's home phone number, which I knew from memory. It rang numerous times before it was picked up, but no one spoke.

"Phuong-Vy," I said.

"Seka," Phuong-Vy sounded relieved.

"What's going on?" I asked.

"I've been getting crank calls tonight. I mean, I'm pretty sure they're crank calls. They could be — Never mind."

"What do you mean? Who could it be?"

Phuong-Vy sighed, giving in. "Tom and I had a fight. He wanted to come over tonight, but I told him you were sleeping over. He got all paranoid, accused me of going out and hiding it. Then the crank calls began, but I don't think it's him. I mean, it can't be. But then I'm also wondering if he's calling to check up on me. Make sure that I'm actually home like I said I would be."

"Fuck, Phuong-Vy, he's gone mental. What are you going to do?"

"Nothing. I mean, I'm not sure if it's him. It could be prank calls."

"Akham's razor. The simplest explanation is always the right one. You wouldn't be suspecting him if you didn't have just cause."

"I know, know. I just thought he was so sweet."

"Hey, did you go to his place?" I asked, remembering our last conversation and how she suspected him of avoiding taking her home.

"Um, no."

"Come on Phuong-Vy, that's a red flag."

"Hey, who are you to talk? Have you been to Ninu's house?"

"Actually, that's where I'm calling from," I said.

"What? What's it like?"

"It's a really huge farm outside of the suburbs. He has his own unit that he built with his dad. His parents are away, so he thought I'd be more comfortable."

"Wow, that's great." Phuong-Vy struggled to inject happiness into her voice.

"That's why I'm calling. I was going to stay over tonight, but now I'm thinking I'll get Ninu to drop me off at your place after dinner."

"Don't you dare. You enjoy your night. Get to know Ninu properly. Find out if he's for real and whether he's worth your time. I'm not in the mood for company tonight. I have some thinking to do about Tom."

"I'm sorry, Phuong-Vy," I said.

"Me too. I was hoping he would be for real."

"I'm going to come over."

"No, you won't," Phuong-Vy snapped. "I'm serious. Stay with Ninu and spend some time with him. Come by tomorrow morning, and we'll have breakfast together. You can tell me all the highlights."

"Deal," I said, feeling relieved. I didn't realise how much I wanted to stay the night with Ninu until it was possibly not going to happen.

I put the phone down and went to the bathroom. After using the facilities, I opened the medicine cabinet, finding muscle ointment, panadol and bandages. Beside Ninu's bed were bedside tables with two framed photos. I lifted one. The middle-aged man with his arm around Ninu's shoulders was his father. The resemblance between the two was striking. His mother was petite and curvy, with curly brown hair and a welcoming smile. His younger brother and sister were a mixture of both parents. They looked a happy family. A whole family. The second frame was a mob of dark-haired relatives who all resembled each other slightly, with Ninu in the middle, smiling happily. A large, happy family. That's what we were before the war. Before my extended family was all killed.

I went to the kitchen and got the potato salad. As I stepped out and entered the patio, the delicious smell of fried vegetables and sizzling meat hit me.

"Smells delicious," I said, placing the potato salad on the table. Ninu had set it with plastic plates and glasses, and silver cutlery.

"Thanks." He flipped the steak and pressed on it.

I walked over to the hot tub in the corner, dipping my hands into the warm water. The hot tub was on a deck, and on the other side was a deep ravine that the house was built on top of. The view from the hot tub was out to rolling hills.

"Do you grow anything?" I asked.

"We grow everything. Behind my unit, there is a field where we have a vegetable patch and a fruit orchard. We grow lots of our food. Even our eggs come from our chickens, and we have a goat to make cheese with."

"Really? You have an entire farm?"

Ninu nodded. "I'll show you after dinner." He placed the steak on a plate and covered it with foil. "It needs to rest, so the juices settle." Then, without hesitation, he draped an arm around my shoulder—casual, effortless, like it was the most natural thing in the world to touch me. I leaned into it, savouring the warmth of his affection, the quiet security it gave me. "My parents bought this land first. It took them five years to save enough to build the house, but while saving, they planted fruit trees and started a garden. That's how they managed to save so much—by making us self-sufficient, just like in Malta. And now, it's just the way we live." His voice was steady, certain. "It's how I want to live, too. I bought land a few kilometres that way, and I'm going to build a house there, somewhere to raise a family. What do you want to do in five years' time?" Ninu asked.

I heard the code in his words. He was looking for commitment. Usually at this point I would freak the fuck out and be planning my exit strategy, but for once I was intrigued and wanting to know plans. I had had none in so long that it was a lovely novelty to think about what my life might be like in five years' time.

"I guess I would be close to finishing my degree. I'd be looking to start my practice or at least buy into a practice, so I had a future."

"Mmm." He put his arms around me. "Having a vet in the family would be the perfect combo."

I held his arms against me, enjoying the feeling of him behind me as we daydreamed of a future.

After dinner, he took me on a tour of his family's house and the extended property. We were in the garage, and a gun was displayed on the wall. "That's my great-grandfather's hunting rifle. It doesn't work anymore. All the guns are locked up." He nodded to a metal cupboard in the corner.

"What do you have guns for?"

"Hunting. My family goes pig hunting in the scrub or shooting. I used to compete when I was young, but I'm not into it anymore."

After dinner, we walked back to his bungalow, and I prepared in the bathroom. As I stepped out of the bathroom in my lavender silk nightie, he was sitting on the edge of the bed, his legs spread, his chest looking impossibly wide in the white t-shirt he wore. I was nervous as I walked to him, my stomach fluttering with butterflies. Even though we'd been together for a few months, this was the first time we were making love deliberately. As I stood between his legs, he put his hands on my waist, his eyes darkening with desire. He kissed my neck, his breath making my skin break out with goose pimples.

"*Int qalbi*," he whispered.

"What does that mean?" I asked.

"You are my heart." He stood and took off his t-shirt, holding me tightly against him, his taut and muscled chest burning me up.

We kissed and sank into bed, our every touch characterised with tenderness. As he entered me, he looked into my eyes, and I lost myself in him. Afterwards, we drifted off to sleep in each other's arms, the first time I'd ever slept with a man. Sometime during the night, I shivered and put on his t-shirt and undies.

I was in Srebrenica, walking uphill on the main road of Marshall Tito, the hospital perched on the hill above me. I needed to get to it and find Ramo. He was lost. I ducked my head down and speed-walked toward the hospital on the hill when a shadow appeared in the sky above me. I looked up, my mouth dropping as I saw the jet plane flying over the town at high speed, so quickly my eyes barely followed its path, white fog enveloping it so that it was like a flying cloud. As it passed, a boom filled the sky. The jet had broken the sound barrier and vanished again. I started running, but within a few metres I was winded. I would never make it to the hospital. As I watched, the white cloud returned. It was coming back. The jet plane was coming back to drop its bomb. I remembered the fragments on the playground, all that was left of the woman and child when a bomb dropped on them. The futility of attempting to outrun a jet plane stalled me, and my feet turned to lead. There was no point. I might as well stop. I should stop and let fate decide.

A woman with short brown hair ran toward me, her arms outstretched, her daughter holding one hand, and her son another. Her face was etched in fear and determination as she ran. The plane was flying behind her. It looked like it was following her, its malevolent form a harbinger of death, getting ready to rain down deadly bombs and sharp pieces of shrapnel that would slice flesh like paper.

"Girl," she shouted, her eyes meeting mine. "Come on."

The woman reached me, swept me up in her wake, and I started running, keeping pace with them. I heard the whistle of the bomb dropping and automatically turned my head to look, but the woman pushed me ahead. The street wobbled with the force of the bomb dropping, and my feet swayed. A dust cloud surrounded us, and we coughed and spluttered as it pushed down our throats. We reached the front of the house. The woman pulled us into the house and slammed the door behind us. The house had been shelled previously. There was a hole in the hallway from a shell that had caved through the roof and left a hole in the floorboards. I followed the children down the hall to the back of the house, which had fared better, and down the stairs to the basement. The house shook around us as the jet plane dropped more bombs, dust rising around me, settling on my hair and clothes, the stairs weaving beneath me. I coughed and spluttered as dust went into my mouth, my balance disrupted, slowing down as I sought sure footing on the steps. The woman placed her hands on my shoulders and urged me down the last step.

"In this corner," the woman pushed us into the basement corner. Next to me was her son, a boy of nine years old with his mother's brown hair and serious eyes, and a girl of five, her hair blonde and wispy. The woman stood before us, as if her very body would shield us from harm. I closed my eyes and held tight to her as her children crowded around me.

I closed my eyes and prayed to a God I didn't believe in, repeating, 'please, please, please,' in my head. A second bomb dropped, a third. The bombs made my ears ring, disrupted my balance, and I opened my eyes, but I couldn't see anything. Dust was floating everywhere. Slowly, it settled and cleared. The woman stared up at the ceiling above us, waiting to see if the roof would collapse in on us and crush us to death. The house held. The planes disappeared.

I looked down at the ground and sighed with relief, and saw the blood seeping into a pool on the ground below the woman.

"They've gone," the woman said after five minutes had passed. Her daughter started crying, her hands held to her ears, the ringing hurting her. The woman turned around, hugged her daughter and soothed her, wincing in pain. She hugged her son to her other side.

I was alone, an interloper. I wanted to hug Ramo, to be held by my mother.

The woman weaved, her knees giving out. I stepped forward and helped to seat her on the stairs.

"Mama, are you okay?" Her little boy cried as he held his mother's hands.

"I'm fine, Munir. Just feeling a little shaky after the bombing." She forced a smile, but her hands were shaking in his.

"What's your name?" The little girl asked, taking her thumb out of her mouth.

"I'm Seka," I said, bobbing down, so we were face-to-face. "What's your name?"

"Munira," she said.

Their mother had done the usual Bosnian tradition of using a name as a template to name all her children. There were many families with a Fikret and Fikreta, Amir and Amira. My father, Fadil, had a sister named Fadila, and my father had wanted to name me Emira to match my brother's name Emir, but Mama had prevailed, naming me Dževahira instead after her favourite cousin who had passed away when she was young. Thankfully Emir had struggled with my name and began calling me Seka, little sister and it stuck.

"I'm Halisa," the woman whispered. She seemed to look worse, rather than better. Her face was pale and shiny.

"Can the two of you get your mother water?" I told Munir and Munira.

After looking at their mother for permission, Munir nodded and took his sister up the stairs.

"Let me see," I asked.

Halisa opened her coat. There was a large bloodstain on her stomach.

"The shrapnel went in through my back," Halisa said. "Can you see it?"

I moved around and saw blood on the back of her jacket, but there was no shrapnel. I came back to the front and helped Halisa lift her top. There was blood seeping out of a wound on the front, a slight edge of shrapnel peeking out through a cut in her stomach.

"I think we need to get you to the hospital," I said. "Can you walk?"

Halisa attempted to stand, but quickly shook her head.

"I'll go find help. You stay here." I climbed up the stairs. Munir and Munira were at the top, holding a glass of water. "I'm going to get help to take your mother to the hospital. Her tummy hurts."

Munir frowned. He opened his mouth to ask questions, but I shook my head, looking at his sister. He nodded.

"Go take water downstairs and be with your Mum while I get help."

They nodded and walked down the stairs. I walked to the front door and opened it.

Screams of pain and anguish rose above the bullets. People appeared on the streets, leaving their basements to help and seek lost people. Two men emerged from the house across the street, carrying a third between them. The man they carried attempted to stand, but couldn't. His head lolled to the side.

The bread van screeched to a halt, and they handed the man over to him.

"Please, help," I said, running toward them. "There's a woman, Halisa. She can't walk. She's been wounded in the stomach."

The two men followed me down the basement stairs. They picked her up between them. She was paler than when I left, looked more wan. As they carried her up the stairs, I saw the stain of blood where she had been sitting.

"Munir, Munira," she cried out weakly.

"Don't worry, I'll bring them to the hospital," I told her, taking them by hand and walking up the stairs with them.

The men deposited Halisa into the van and continued running up the street as the van sped away.

"Your mother will be all right," I told the children as we walked. "We'll meet her at the hospital."

Munira looked at me with trusting brown eyes and nodded mutely. Munir didn't look convinced. I saw him looking at the blood stain where his mother had been sitting. He knew something was wrong.

We continued walking. The footpaths were filled with the wounded, all heading in the same direction, toward the hospital. As we got closer, there were more and more people; some were carrying others, and those who could walk were traipsing with an uncertain gait. I passed a woman who was holding a bleeding arm, droplets of blood marking her passage. A man was pushing a wheelbarrow with a screaming man who had half a leg missing. A man ran with a child in his arms, the child's head limply bouncing against his arm. We were an army of the broken.

"Seka, Seka," someone shook me awake. I opened my eyes and saw I was in a field, Ninu standing in front of me in his boxer shorts.

"What happened?" I asked, looking around the Australian landscape. I was just in Srebrenica. How did I get to Australia?

"You sleepwalked."

I winced as the pain in my feet penetrated. I looked behind me and saw his house was so far away, it was tiny in the distance.

"I don't remember." An aeroplane passed overhead, and I flinched, shielding my face as I screamed.

"It's okay. It's just a plane. We're near the airport." Ninu held me tightly while I shivered. I looked where he was pointing and saw metal glinting in the distance, a tower.

"Come on, let's get back." He gently walked with me back to the house.

I looked down at my feet, avoiding the sharp rocks, feeling discombobulated.

"I must have been dreaming," I murmured. "I dreamed I was in Srebrenica when the bomb fell." And then, I remembered the woman.

"It's okay." Ninu had his arm around me, and we slowly walked together as I trembled. When we got to his flat, he turned on the hose and washed our feet. I winced as the water hit my feet. He sat me down and picked out the cactus embedded there. "I have to treat this." He returned with antiseptic and gauze, ministering to my feet.

"I should have died that day," I told him. "If it weren't for that woman, I would have. I just froze. She died when we got to the hospital, her two children becoming orphans. She'd saved my life."

Ninu looked at me with concern. He gently hugged me. "You're safe now."

His words rang hollow. I never felt safe. I always felt like I was five minutes from death. The years we'd spent in Australia, I'd expected to die at any moment. Last night was the first time I'd allowed myself to feel a future, and then I'd had a dream. Was it an omen or just my fucked up subconscious warning me not to let my guard down?

9-Bus

Ninu walked me to Phuong-Vy's door and waited while I knocked. She answered wearing a tracksuit, her eyes red-rimmed and her face splotched.

"What happened?" I hugged her. Ninu hung back, holding a paper bag with toasted croissants and a coffee.

"Tom came by this morning at 6 am. When he saw you didn't sleep over, he became suspicious. He was almost paranoid, as if I told him you were staying here so he couldn't come over. We had a fight. Our first proper fight." Phuong-Vy was crying as she talked.

I held her tightly until she calmed down a few moments later.

"Sorry for being such a drama queen," Phuong-Vy said, stepping away. "Come in Ninu." She gestured for him to come inside as she wiped her eyes.

"It's okay. I don't want to intrude on your girl talk." He placed the bag and coffee on the kitchen table, leaned in, and kissed me, his eyes holding mine as he smiled sweetly.

A melting sensation filled me.

"See you later," he said.

"See you." I watched him go, my eyes lingering on his backside as he walked.

"Wow, so that's how things went last night." She opened the paper bag and took out a croissant, breaking it apart and eating it. "Spill all the details."

I smiled, my cheeks feeling warm.

"Are you blushing?" Phuong-Vy exclaimed, leaning in for a closer look.

"No, I'm not." I turned away, calming myself with a deep breath. "He makes me feel safe. There are no games. He knows what he wants and is not afraid to go after it." As I spoke, I looked out the window.

"Are you afraid?" she asked.

"When am I not afraid? It's like if I allow myself to want something, it will be taken away from me. Don't you feel like that?"

"A little. But I also feel like I don't know how long I have, so I want to live while I can. Experience everything there is to experience." She took a sip of her coffee.

"But aren't you scared of loving someone and having them die?"

"Yes, but I'm also scared of never loving someone and spending my whole life half a person."

Her words hit me like a bullet. Was that I was doing? Living half a life because I was too scared to open myself up?

"Ninu wants children?"

"What do you want?"

"I don't know. I know I don't want children. I don't want anything that ties me down—anything that makes me vulnerable."

"Then you need to let him go." She said off-hand, like she was talking about a pair of shoes.

"What? No, we're having fun." My blood pressure surged as she dismissed him out of hand.

"No, you're having fun. You said it yourself. He wants commitment. He doesn't want to play games. And you know what you don't want. You know you don't want children or marriage. So you need to let him go."

Why was she being such a bitch?

"I don't want to," I snapped.

"I guess you're not certain what you want, and that's okay. You're only 22. You have time to figure things out." She smiled and waggled her eyebrows.

"You're such an asshole," I said, tossing my half-eaten croissant at her.

"That's right baby, reverse psychology. You know I got that good shit from my therapist."

"I hate you," I muttered.

"No, you don't. You love me, and I love you." She handed me the croissant back.

I brushed off the couch lint and took another bite. I never understood the Aussie obsession with the five-second rule—acting like food was instantly contaminated the moment it touched the ground. I wanted that croissant, and a little dirt wouldn't kill me. Nothing would, if the food I'd scavenged from the garbage in Srebrenica hadn't.

"Technically, you and Ninu only had your first date last night. You need to give yourself time to see where this leads."

"Okay, enough about me and Ninu. What about you and Tom?"

"I don't know. He was so insecure. It was a side I didn't expect to see from him." She pushed her hair over her shoulder.

We heard footsteps coming toward her front door. She pushed down the blind and peered out. She looked over my shoulder and gasped, before running to the door.

"I'm so sorry, baby," Tom's voice said when she opened the door, holding a huge bouquet in front of him. "Do you forgive me?"

"Oh, wow. They're so beautiful." She teared up and stepped outside. I saw her partial body as the two of them embraced, and heard the sounds of kissing.

"And that's my cue to leave." I picked up my bag and walked toward the door.

"No, you don't have to leave," Phuong-Vy said, her eyes on Tom.

"I need to get home, anyway. My Mum is expecting me."

I walked to the train station with a lightness in my step. Things were looking up. Life was full of possibilities, the possibilities of romance, as well as retribution. A delicious feeling of anticipation filled me as I plotted.

A week later, on a Tuesday, work called with an extra shift, which I would always take, but today I had other plans. I caught the bus to Footscray and waited for his bus to arrive. I wasn't wearing a disguise and was dressed in jeans and a top. Today, I wanted him to know it was me.

As I stepped on, I inserted my ticket into the machine. He stared out the windshield as he waited for the bus to fill. "Hello Miroslav," I said in our language, waving at him.

"Hello Zora." He smiled as he turned to look at me.

"I was wondering if I'd see you today," I said, offering a small smile. "I'm heading to Highpoint to meet my friends and remembered you drive this bus." I figured it was best to put his mind at ease.

"Ah."

I sat on the bus seat near the front door, directly in his line of sight. I wanted to talk to him on this trip.

"I'm not great on buses—motion sickness. I have to sit at the front." I dropped my backpack onto the seat beside me, a silent deterrent for anyone thinking of sitting down. "How's Lux doing?" I asked.

"Good. Always bugging me for walks. It falls to me now that my girls aren't home, but I get tired after working all day."

"How old are your daughters?" I asked, seizing on the opportunity to ask. I had twenty minutes until we reached the end of the line, and I had to milk this for every bit of information.

"They're 16 and 14," Miroslav said, checking the rearview mirror as he pulled out of the bay.

"How are they enjoying being in Australia?"

"Good, good. They're in Queensland at the moment, visiting my wife's sister."

"That's wonderful. So you have more family here."

"Me, no. My parents were killed in the war when my village was attacked. My sister lives in Germany. But my wife's sister came to Australia too. They moved to Queensland because it's warmer."

"Yes, I don't like this Melbourne weather at all. What do the Aussies say—just wait five minutes and the weather will change."

Miroslav laughed. "When we came, we were told we'd be coming to Queensland too, so I gave away all my winter jackets to friends in Serbia. And when we arrived in July, it was the heart of winter here, and I nearly got pneumonia."

We both laughed.

"In English class, the teacher served us Vegemite on toast, calling it an Aussie delicacy. I nearly gagged on the spot. For a moment, I thought she was playing a prank on us." Even now, I remember the sharp bitterness hitting my throat, my gag reflex kicking in.

We laughed together, and for a moment, I forgot who I was and what I was here to do. We were two former Yugoslavs sharing war stories about migrating and acclimating to a new culture. He turned at the traffic light, and the sunlight streamed into the bus. I caught sight of my reflection in the windshield before me, the short bobbed hair, the blue eyes glinting in a mirror face that was mine, but wasn't, and remembered.

He pulled up at the next stop, and two middle-aged women got in, greeting Miroslav by name. He greeted them by name. They sat on the seat behind him.

"How are Gordana and the girls in Queensland?" The brunette with the black headscarf asked.

"They're good."

"When are they coming back?" Black Headscarf asked.

"Soon. Soon."

"They've been there for three months now?" The one with red permed hair asked.

"Maybe, I'm not sure."

"The girls have missed a lot of school." Red Perm said.

"They're attending school over there," he said.

The two women exchanged a glance.

"Are you sure they're visiting? It sounds like Gordana's left you," Black Headscarf said.

There was a long silence as Mirsoslav said nothing, his face flushing red.

The women looked at each other in consternation.

"Tell Gordana hello when you speak to her," Red Perm said.

"Of course," Miroslav nodded.

"Did you read this?" Red Perm said, taking out a newspaper. She held it up for her seatmate to see. It was the Serb newspaper I'd bought at Psarakos a few weeks ago when I first spotted him.

Her seatmate shook her head. Red Perm licked her finger and turned the well-worn pages. "Look at this." She turned to the article about the Srebrenica memorial, and nausea began churning through me.

"It says that there was no massacre in Srebrenica. That the Muslims are just pretending to get international sympathy."

"I believe it. Of course those Balije are pretending."

"There is a witness, Radojka, who saw one of her former neighbours. Do you know her?" she asked her seatmate, who shook her head. "What about you, Miroslav? Do you know Radojka?"

"Radojka Živković?" Miroslav asked.

Red Perm peered closer at the newspaper, confirming the surname before nodding.

"I know her. She's blind as a bat. She got on the bus last week and thought I was Stanko, who drives the 86 bus."

"What does Stanko look like?" Red Perm asked, leaning closer to the bus driver.

"He's fat and bold."

Black Scarf and Red Perm chortled. "Sounds like you were insulted because she didn't see how handsome you are."

"Yes, I was insulted," Miroslav said. "With this head of hair."

"There's another witness—a Nemanja Tomić. Do you know him?" she asked them both.

They all shook their heads.

"He saw his neighbour too."

As I listened to them speak, I clutched the metal bar, nausea churning through me. I wanted to get up and beat their skulls into their heads, but I had to remain calm. I had to play the part of the Serb girl.

I looked over, and Silver Cross looked angry, his face red beneath his beard.

"What about you Miroslav? You were in Srebrenica. Was there a massacre?" The two women stared at him as they waited.

I held my breath, gripping the bar in front of me hard.

There was a long pause before Miroslav replied. "I was there with the Serb army, and we placed all the residents on buses, sent them safely to the free territory."

"That was just the women and children. What happened to the men?" I demanded in our language, the words bursting out of me in a rush.

The two women looked at me with surprise. They hadn't realised I understood their conversation.

"We put them on buses too," Miroslav said.

I wanted to jump in and ask more questions, but before I could, Miroslav changed the conversation, asking Red Perm about her husband and his back injury.

"He's doing well. He's going back to work next week, the doctor said," Red Perm said.

"Glad to hear it," Miroslav said.

"And who are you?" Black Scarf asked me.

"Zora Đokić," I answered.

They waited for more information.

"Slobodan Đokić is my father."

They nodded. With shaking hands, I took a book out of my backpack, lifting it in front of me, and pretending to read to end the conversation.

The women quietened down, talking about their husbands behind me. I stared at the page, the words swimming before me, fighting to keep my composure.

The bus pulled up at a stop, and people got on the bus and continued down the aisle.

"This is your stop," Miroslav said.

I looked up from my book and saw we were at Highpoint, where I'd told him I was getting off. If I didn't get off, he'd be suspicious.

"Thanks." I forced a smile as I got off.

I stepped off the bus and heard the doors close behind me. The bus departed from the bay and drove away. I started shaking, my legs trembling as the tears burst out of me. I fell to my knees at the bus stop.

"Are you all right, dearie?" An elderly Anglo woman asked, bending over me.

I couldn't speak. I was crying so hard. She took me in her arms and held me tightly. "I know, it's hard. Sometimes we just have to get it out."

She offered me her bottle of water. "Here, take a drink. Are you better?"

I nodded, even though it wasn't true. I would never be better, not while Miroslav was enjoying his life, while my father and Ramo rotted somewhere, forever lost.

I thanked the woman, caught the tram to the city, and then home, feeling like someone had run over me with a truck. I felt myself sinking as I looked out the window and saw the passing landscape. I fell asleep. Ramo sat next to me on the tram.

My heart gladdened as his blonde hair sparkled in the sunlight streaming through the tram window.

"What are you going to do now?" His hand, wearing the matching eternity ring, gripped mine.

A feeling of safety filled me. He was here.

"I'm going to get the truth." I gripped his hand tighter, in awe that I could feel his warm palm against mine.

"What truth?" he asked.

I couldn't remember. What truth was I looking for? What did I need to find?

"I want to find you." As I remembered my mission, he dissipated, fading from sight. The warmth of his palm against mine faded.

I woke up, looking at my hand. The seat beside me was empty. I wiped the tears as I sat straighter. These dreams in which I forgot he was dead were the worst. When I woke up and remembered he was gone, it was like I was losing him all over again.

I fixed my focus on Miroslav and the fury burning inside me. He had admitted he was in Srebrenica. He knew the truth—knew exactly what had happened—and still, he lied. Clinging to his loyalty to Great Serbia, he spread the deceit, denying the genocide. He had to pay for what he had done.

I clenched my fists as I rifled through ideas about how to enact my revenge. His weak spot was his love for Lux. That was the quickest way to hurt him. I had to take away what he loved.

10-Dopelganger

I stood outside his house, rage burning through me. I wanted Miroslav to suffer, and Lux was the key. All I had to do was steal his beloved pet from him and remove his microchip so Lux couldn't be traced. I watched Miroslav leave for work and waited another 20 minutes to ensure the coast was clear before walking past the house and ducking into the front yard.

"Hello Lux," I said as I approached the gate.

Recognising my voice, Lux jumped up, pushing his nose in the gap between the fence, his tongue lolling as he was happy to see me.

I patted him, my hand on the gate. If I took him, I would remove the microchip so the rangers couldn't return him, but then what? Miroslav would search all the shelters looking for him, and if Lux was there, he would get him back.

I had to find a way for Lux to never be found by Miroslav. I could take him to a shelter somewhere in the country, where it would never occur to Miroslav to look. Then there was a chance that Lux would be euthanised when no one claimed him.

I looked into Lux's big brown eyes, filled with trust and happiness. I couldn't do it. I couldn't make an innocent animal suffer just to hurt Miroslav.

I handed Lux the treat I had in my pocket. "Good boy." I patted him on the head and left, feeling like a coward. I should show Miroslav no mercy, no matter the consequences, but instead, I was a victim of my conscience.

The next day, I was at work on my break with Ninu. We were behind the clinic, where no one could see us, taking a few minutes to cuddle.

"It's my twenty-fifth birthday in a few weeks," he said, his arms firm around me.

"Are you angling for a special birthday present?" I looked up and suggestively raised my eyebrows.

He laughed. "My parents are throwing a birthday party for the family. I want you to come."

"Oh, wow." I gulped, nervous at the prospect of declaring ourselves a couple publicly.

"It will be just my close family and friends. Nothing big." He looked at me with eager eyes.

I remembered my conversation with Phuong-Vy. I had to give this relationship a chance. Let it play out and see what happens.

"I'd love to come to your birthday party."

Ninu smiled. "My parents are going to love you."

He hugged me, and I let myself sink against his chest. I didn't share his optimism, but that was a problem for another day. I felt drained, restless. Sleep had become a battleground, my mind churning through the same dark thoughts every night—how to make Miroslav suffer. I wanted him in pain.

Terrible ideas had come and gone, each more reckless than the last. Arson. Poisoning. Plans formed and unravelled, discarded before they could take root.But the hunger for revenge remained.

"I'm so glad you said yes. It's the only good thing that's happened to me today."

"Why are you having a bad day?"

Ninu tensed beneath my touch. "It gets to me when the owners don't make sure their dogs can't escape. This dog that I collected from the road today, I'd picked him up three times before. Three times, but the owners wouldn't spend the money on shoring up the fence so that he couldn't jump. Even though I told them it was a matter of time until he was killed."

"I'm so sorry." I squeezed him tighter, both my arms on his stiff back.

"I think it gets to me because my dog Brownie looked exactly like this one, a classic German Shepherd. All beautiful elegance and patches of brown." Ninu stroked his hands through my hair. "Brownie had so much space to roam at my house. A snake took him."

"A German Shepherd? Is it a boy?" I asked, my plan clicking into place.

"Yes." Ninu sighed heavily, sticking his head into my neck. "Now, I've got to take him to the kennels where the owners will pick him up." He sounded defeated and forlorn.

"You shouldn't have to do that. Why don't you leave him here, and I'll get the owners to come and get him?" I leaned back in his arms and looked at his face.

"It's not fair. It's my job." Ninu attempted a stoic face.

"Yes, and it's mine too. And sometimes you just need to catch a break, so today is your turn to be taken care of." I placed my hands on his cheeks and gently kissed him. "Let's go to the truck, and I'll take him." I grabbed his arm and dragged him to the truck, wearing a huge grin that Ninu couldn't see.

He pulled me to a stop, and I wiped the grin off my face before looking at him seriously.

"You're a top girl." Ninu looked at me with tears glistening in his dark eyelashes. "You really get me."

Guilt bit me. Ninu thought I was doing this because I was concerned about him. I'd like to think that if it weren't for my plan, I would show him the same concern and consideration, but I knew I probably wouldn't. A hardness within me didn't account for other people's weakness. I would tell him to harden up and do what must be done. After all, everyone dies at some point.

I leaned in and kissed him before I could think too much about it. Did it really matter that my kindness was selfish, that I was only doing it because it served me? It was still a kind act. I told myself I didn't believe the lie, but that didn't matter. I finally had my chance for retribution—my pesky conscience could take a hike.

I helped Ninu carry the dead German Shepherd to our freezer and took the paperwork from him. I walked him back to the council truck and kissed him through the window. "Damn, I forgot to ask you, can I borrow your truck tonight? Mama bought some furniture and needs help to bring it home."

"Do you want me to come and help?"

I shook my head. "No, my mother would forbid me from seeing you if she met you. You're not Muslim, remember?"

"Oh, okay. I'll drop the truck off later and get my cousin to pick me up from here."

"Thanks." I pecked him on the cheek and left.

As I worked the rest of the afternoon, I prepared all the steps I had to follow for my plan to succeed. After my shift ended, I got in Ninu's truck and drove to Miroslav's house, parking one street away.

I put on Ninu's hoodie, which was in the passenger seat, and walked past Miroslav's house. The windows were lit up, and Lux barked as I walked past. He was home. This would be riskier than I thought, but it had to be done. I'd already called home and told Mama I would be sleeping at Phuong-Vy's. I'd called Phuong-Vy to check in so she would cover for me. She'd been preoccupied with Tom there. They'd been spending every minute together, and she'd cancelled two lunch dates in the past week. He was monopolising her attention, and she was so caught up in a love bubble she didn't notice it, but that was a problem for another time.

I drove the truck a few blocks to where there was a park. Locked the windows and pushed the seat down. I needed to sleep now because I had a busy night ahead of me. I felt wired awake, my brain ticking over everything, but somehow sheer exhaustion took me under. When I opened my eyes, the truck's cab had cooled, and I felt chilled. I sat up and lifted the seat. The suburban street around me was deserted. I looked at the clock. It was 1 o'clock. Hopefully, now would be a good time.

I turned over the truck and drove down Miroslav's street. It was quiet, and most houses were dark, with one at the beginning of the street with light around the window—a night owl. I parked the truck a few houses up and walked back to Miroslav's gate.

"Hey, Lux, it's me," I spoke softly from the neighbour's fence, just enough to keep him from barking. The trick worked. Lux perked up, ears pricked, his front paws resting on the gate as he peered at me. "I'm here, buddy." I gave him the pig's ears he loved, watching as he chewed contentedly. Moving quickly, I unlatched the side gate, clipped on his lead, and strode back to the truck. Lux trotted beside me, tail wagging, oblivious to the weight pressing on my chest. At Ninu's truck, I guided Lux through the driver's seat and into the passenger side. He settled in without hesitation. I climbed in, started the engine, and pulled away, my shoulders loosening slightly. The most dangerous part was over. Now came the hardest part—the endurance test.

I drove back to the vet clinic. The carpark was deserted, the front lights of the reception dark. I used my keys and opened it, quickly undoing the alarm, and led Lux to the surgery room. His ears were flattened, and his tail stopped wagging. He didn't like the vet.

"It's okay buddy. You won't be in any pain." I found a syringe and pinched his flesh together before injecting him in the neck. He whimpered quickly, but didn't move away. I patted him gently all over, monitoring the clock. I needed at least ten minutes to be safe.

I got the scalpel and made a small nick on Lux's neck, pinching out the microchip. "There, all done." I put the microchip onto the tray and rubbed antiseptic on the area I had nicked. "You'll be fine."

I attached Lux to the table and went to the back, where the carcass was. It was frozen and hard to manoeuvre out of the freezer. The dog's jaw was broken, and an eye was hanging from the socket. I covered it with a paper towel and used a scalpel to cut out the microchip. I inserted Lux's microchip into the dog.

After I returned the dog to the freezer, I sat on the floor. Lux came over and lay his head on my lap. "I'm so sorry," I cried, tears dripping onto his neck. "But I promise you, you'll have an even better owner and a better life."

I was going to do it again? Do a terrible thing for a greater good. I could stop this, right here, right now. I didn't have to go through with it.

"Get up. Undo it," I told myself, but my legs wouldn't move. I had to play this out.

"Let's go."

I turned off the lights and locked up the clinic before getting in the truck with Lux. I drove us home. Mama and Emir were used to me bringing strays for a few days until I could find the owner, and wouldn't blink an eye to find a dog in the backyard.

I secured Lux's lead to the fence, filled a water bowl and set it on the patio's concrete. Grabbing another bowl, I poured some dry dog food and placed it beside him. Settling into a chair, I gazed up at the moon, a quiet calm washing over me. The thought of Miroslav waking to an empty backyard in the morning sent a wave of satisfaction through me. Lux finished his meal, then curled up at my feet, his warmth grounding me in the moment.

"Okay, I've got to go to bed." I nudged him with my toes.

He stood. I walked to the sliding doors and opened it. Lux followed, nudging his head into the opening.

"You stay here."

He cocked his head at me, his face showing confusion and sadness. I closed the sliding door. He whimpered behind me; the sound tugging my heart.

"Shhh," I hissed.

He lay on the ground in a supplicant pose, looking at me with his gentle brown eyes. I was leaving him outside to sleep, something Miroslav did every night. Yes, but that was in his own home, his own backyard, with his beloved owner.

"It's okay. I'll take care of you. Ninu is such a good guy; he'll love you so much. We just have to wait a week until his birthday so that you can be his present."

I closed the door, and Lux whimpered again. I sighed in frustration.

"Fine, you win." I unclipped his lead and let him come into the house. He padded through the living room beside me and to my bedroom. I pointed to the floor, and Lux lay next to the bed while I lay on the bed in my clothes, exhaustion weighing me down. I was drifting to sleep when I felt Lux jump up beside me. He curled up against my back, warming me, and I drifted off to the most peaceful sleep I'd had in months.

My bedroom door opened, waking me. Mama said my name and then screamed.

I sat up in bed, looking around with fear.

"What is that doing here?" Mama demanded, pointing at Lux, sitting on the floor, looking at her with his ears pointed.

"He's going to stay here for a few days while I find his owner." I stretched and yawned.

"You know the rules, Seka."

"Sorry, Mama." I stood and led Lux out of my bedroom. Pets belonged outside only. They were never to pass the threshold of the house. Now, Mama would make me scrub the house from top to bottom to remove any evidence of Lux.

"Another customer." As Lux and I walked past, Emir was sitting at the kitchen table reading the newspaper.

I opened the sliding door and let Lux out. He looked at me plaintively.

"Marsh," Mama said firmly, using the Bosnian word to get lost.

Recognising her tone or the word, Lux bounded away from the sliding door and began sniffing the backyard, checking the boundaries of his domain.

"I don't want to see that animal back in this house. And after breakfast, you can get out the vacuum cleaner and make sure there's no fur in the house."

"Yes, Mama." I sat down to eat breakfast, chastened. It was 9 o'clock, and I felt refreshed even though I'd only slept five hours. There was nothing like sheer joy to lift one's spirits.

As I sipped my tea, I imagined Miroslav's face as he realised Lux wasn't in the yard. The fear as he began looking for him up and down the streets. The sickening panic in the pit of his stomach as he wondered what had happened to his beloved pet. Did a crime gang steal him so he could be in an illegal fight? Was he hit by a car?

"What are you so happy about?" Emir asked, peering at me over his newspaper.

"Just stuff."

He looked to see that Mama wasn't in earshot. "My mate Enes said he saw you kissing a dark-haired guy in front of the vet clinic."

Fuck. I hated the ethnic network and the way they all spied on everyone and reported it back.

"So." I took a sip of tea.

"Anyone I know?" he asked.

I knew what this was code for. He wanted to know if Ninu was Muslim.

"You don't know him." I took a bite of toast, hoping he'd drop it.

"Are you going to bring him home for Mum to meet?"

"It's early days." I attempted to evade his question.

His hands crumpled the newspaper. "You know what it would do to Mama if she knew you were dating someone who wasn't Muslim?"

"This is none of your business," I snapped.

"Shhh." He looked at the hallway to see if Mama had heard me shouting.

"I'm just warning you that there's talk, that's all. And eventually Mama will hear it." He lifted the newspaper back in front of his face.

"What about you? Are you dating any suitable young Bosnian women?" I demanded.

"No, nothing yet." He kept reading.

"That's interesting. A young man your age."

He said nothing. I suspected he did the same thing as me, dated whoever he wanted to, regardless of ethnic background. But on the surface, he was the perfect Muslim boy: dressed modestly, prayed daily, attended the mosque every Friday, and lived a chaste life.

Mama entered, dragging the vacuum cleaner behind her. "When you finish breakfast, you can start here and work your way through the house."

I restrained a groan. Emir finished breakfast and left the house. He was the boy, therefore he was exempt from helping with cleaning the house. That was the domain of females and the responsibility of me and my mother. The sexism pissed me off, but there was no point bringing it up.

As I vacuumed, Lux watched me through the sliding door. "This is all your fault," I muttered. He wagged his tail at me.

11-Memento

I was filing at the vet clinic while Kesha talked on the phone. When I heard her repeat the name Zora Đokić, I ran toward her, holding out my hand.

"Here she is now." Kesha handed me the phone.

I turned away as I answered. There was only one person who would call the clinic using that name.

"Zora, it's Miroslav," he said, his voice tight. "Lux is missing. I was wondering if he's at your clinic."

My stomach clenched, but I kept my tone even. "No, I'm so sorry, Miroslav. He's not here."

He exhaled heavily into the phone. "It's been a week."

"Have you checked the shelters?" I asked, forcing down the smile threatening to surface. Kesha was listening.

"Yes. I contacted all the councils."

"Maybe you could put up flyers. I'd be happy to help." This was my opening—my chance to insert myself into his life, to see how much he was really suffering.

"I don't have a photo," he admitted. "My wife took all the albums when she left."

So the women on the bus were right—his wife had left him. The realisation sent a spark through me. "Actually, I have a photo," I said, my voice soft with just the right touch of sympathy. "I took one that day. We like to keep records of our success stories—when pets and owners are reunited. There aren't many."

"You have a photo?" His voice lifted with hope.

"Sure. I can come over, and we can put up flyers in your neighbourhood. Someone might have seen him. Maybe someone even has him in their backyard."

"Thank you, Zora. This means so much."

"We have to look out for each other."

We set a time for tomorrow, and I hung up, plotting how to use this to my advantage.

"You're going above and beyond," Kesha said from behind me.

"I know. I feel so sorry for him. His wife left him and took his children. His dog was all he had."

"And he's not even your countryman. If there were more people like you, then that war wouldn't have happened that killed your country." Kesha patted me on the shoulder.

I nodded, momentary guilt fluttering in my stomach, before quickly being chased by delight. Kesha didn't know what she was talking about. It was men like Miroslav who had killed my country, and now it was his turn to pay. All my plans were coming to fruition. I could now see close up and personal the pain he was suffering from the loss of his beloved dog.

"I've just got to run an errand," I told Kesha. I ran out of the clinic and into the taxi that had pulled up. I told the taxi driver to drive me home and wait a few minutes after I rattled off the address.

He stopped in front of my house, and I unlocked my front door, thankful no one else was home. I was carrying the camera from work, which we used to take photos of pets or injuries for posterity. As I walked across the living room, Lux appeared in front of the sliding doors, wagging his tail.

I stepped out and greeted him. I scanned the backyard, looking for an unobtrusive corner to photograph him. There was a bare corner against the wooden fence. I walked Lux there and got him to sit down. He watched me with his head cocked as I took photographs of him.

"Good boy." I patted his head and sprinted back into the house and to the taxi.

When I returned to work, I spent the afternoon preparing a flyer, and when Kesha went on break, I printed 50 copies that I stashed in my purse. Hanging these up would give me ample time to bond with Miroslav. Who said a good deed never paid off?

I arrived at his house wearing my jeans and a t-shirt. I was both excited and full of trepidation. Miroslav opened the door before I knocked. He must have been watching from the living room and saw me.

"Welcome, Zora," he said, stepping aside and showing me through.

I walked into the hallway, and the living room was the first door on the left. It was strange looking out the window from which I had spied on him for so long. There was something discombobulating about being on the inside when I was outside for so long.

I walked in, looking around the house. We walked down a long hallway into a living room, with a sliding door leading to the kitchen. It was bare, dishevelled. Obviously, without a woman's touch. There were photo frames on a wall cabinet opposite the couch. Miroslav with two young girls, his wife smiling and blonde.

"Please, take a seat." He held out his hand to the green patterned couch, the fabric faded and frayed. "My wife took all the furniture when she moved to Queensland, and I bought these at a second-hand op shop." He rubbed the back of his neck, his face flushed with embarrassment.

"Thank you." I sat. "We're still furnishing our house. When we first arrived, we had a crate as a coffee table."

Miroslav smiled, his embarrassment fading. The reality of being a refugee was that we needed time to establish ourselves. Most of us had arrived in Australia with little more than a bag of clothes, all our mementos left behind to rot and ruin.

"I brought these." I took the posters out of my bag and handed them over.

Miroslav looked at the poster. I'd featured Lux prominently in the centre. He nodded his head, his eyelashes glistening.

"I brought this photo too." I handed him the photo I'd had printed of Lux on his haunches, tongue lolling, looking like he was smiling.

He took it and traced Lux before walking to the shelf above the heater. There was a photo of him in his Australian bus uniform, a proud photograph of his achievement in getting employment in his actual profession when so many had to toil in factories.

His voice was thick with emotion. "He was such a good dog."

"He was. He was so friendly and gentle. Your daughters must have loved having him around."

"They did." He took the photo out and replaced it with Lux, placing it in the centre of the shelf. "They loved having a puppy to shower their love and affection on. My wife wasn't keen. We had a dog in Yugoslavia. We had to let him go to give him a chance to survive when we were chased out of our village."

I remembered the dogs in Srebrenica during the war—once coddled, fed every day, then abandoned to fend for themselves. They lived off scraps, cold, hungry, and bedraggled, scavenging through the ruins of a shattered world. On the day of the playground massacre—when Serb shells rained down on a schoolyard filled with families, killing so many—I had seen a German Shepherd dart away, something clutched in its jaws. A severed hand. Was it his? The thought twisted inside me, but I shoved it down, along with the anger threatening to rise. I was Zora.

"We had a dog too. A tornjak called Bobby," I told Miroslav. "Thankfully, he passed away a year before the war. Tata wanted another one, but he only wanted a tornjak from his home village, and we were waiting for a litter." I remembered Zora's Bosnian Shepherd dog. He was so large, with white fluffy fur and patches of brown. We'd used him in our games, pretending he was a horse we rode into battle when we played cowboys. "I'm glad we didn't get another one. It was so terrible what happened to the dogs afterwards."

Miroslav nodded. "I saw some of them when I was in the army. They were starving, half mad from the noise of war. They learned to view humans as enemies or food. A starving dog attacked my friend while we were sleeping, hoping he was dying. I was sure this Lux would live to an old age. There was no war, and he would be safe and fed. That's what I told my wife when she resisted. I should have realised the name Lux was cursed. There is no peace for him."

"He was too curious for his own good. Once he figured out how to get out of the yard and go exploring, he was his own worst enemy."

"I know. I tried to figure it out. I even installed another bolt, but still, he found a way out. He must have learned to jump over it." Miroslav looked out the window and toward the side gate.

I quickly diverted the topic, not wanting him to think too much about how Lux had gotten out.

"Fingers crossed our posters will help find him."

"Would you like a coffee?" His voice was guttural, and he kept his back to me.

I should have felt happy that he was crying. Instead, guilt was pricking me again. "Yes, please."

He nodded and walked through the sliding door to the kitchen. I inspected the living room around me. What could I use here to my advantage? I noticed the keys were in a bowl on the shelf next to the photo of Lux. I rubbed my lip as a thought formed.

I smelled the coffee from the living room. He was making the typical Yugoslav coffee, thick as mud, glistening in the sun, and as bitter as charcoal. I hated this coffee and did everything possible to avoid drinking it, but I wasn't me, Seka. I was Zora. Zora loved our thick coffee.

He prepared it on the stove, boiling the thick coffee in a *džezva*, a long-necked coffee pot with a long handle. The coffee frothed and glistened on top before he placed it on a tray. He brought the tray over, and I saw he'd already boiled milk with thick blobs of cream floating on top. I especially hated the cream in coffee. Miroslav poured coffee in a *fildžan*, a small demitasse coffee cup, and ladled in the milk, choosing the thick pieces of cream that were usually so desired in our homeland.

I smiled, pretending I was happy to see it floating in my coffee. Miroslav poured himself a cup and took a sip. I broke a sugar cube, placed a piece in my mouth, and then drank a sip of coffee. The sugar barely made it palatable as it washed down. I had to fight not to gag on the cream as I swallowed.

He took out a cigarette packet from his shirt pocket. "Would you like one?" he offered out of politeness.

I reached for it without thinking. A good Yugoslav girl doesn't smoke, but fuck it, I needed something to centre me. He didn't react, just held out the lighter and lit up. There was something so natural about each holding a cup with hot coffee in one hand, a cigarette clutched in the other. As we alternated between lifting the cigarette to our mouths to suck at the filter, and lifting the cup to their lips to sip coffee, I had a sense of deja vu, of being out of place and out of time. I was back in Bosnia before the war, before there were ethnic divisions, before genocide was an everyday term, and we were one.

The smoke dissipated, and as I caught sight of Miroslav, I thudded back down to earth and the night he entered my life, his face cast in shadow, his body a threat to me.

"I was wondering if we could talk about Srebrenica."

Miroslav was shaking his head before I even finished the sentence. "That's a hard story."

"I've been wondering if my best friend survived. Seka and I grew up together. Our families lived next door, and our fathers were best friends. I heard her father died at Potočari, but if it's a Muslim lie, then she's lying, too."

Miroslav got up and went to the wall cabinet behind us, taking out a bottle of rakija. He poured himself a shot glass and slugged it back, followed by a coffee.

He was quiet for so long, I thought he wouldn't answer.

"They're not lying."

"What happened?" I waited, hoping the silence would prod a confession from him. "My friend deserves to bury her father."

"You think me talking will help your friend, help anyone? There is no help for any of us."

I eyed the *džezva*. I wanted to throw the hot coffee on him. He was a self-serving, drunken coward. He didn't want to face up to the truth of what he did.

"My Gordana left me. I don't want to talk about this."

I opened my mouth to ask more questions.

"No." He almost shouted.

I subsided. I had to ease off. At this rate, I would alienate him and jeopardise my entire plan.

"Sorry, I didn't mean to push. I'm just curious. Have your girls been to many amusement parks in Queensland?"

I listened with half an ear as he took my lead to engage in small talk, while I wrestled with my rage.

"Let's go put those posters up." I finished my coffee and returned my saucer and *fildžan* to the tray.

He stood with the tray.

"Do you mind if I use your toilet?" I asked.

"Down the hallway. Last door to your left."

I nodded and walked down the hall. His house had three bedrooms, and they all opened from the hallway. His bedroom had a bedroom suite, the double bed made. What were his daughter's rooms were empty. One had boxes stacked in the corner, the other had a few plastic bags, but was empty. I pushed the door open to the bathroom. There was a bath with a shower over it, a toilet to the left, and a vanity. I tiptoed to the bedroom across. It was a sliding window with a piece of wood inserted into the groove to stop a robber from sliding it open from the outside. I gently popped the wood out, placed it on the floor, and slid the window slightly open. I returned to the bathroom, pressed the toilet to flush, and turned on the tap.

As I came back down the hallway, Miroslav was waiting by the front door. I stepped out before him and waited while he locked the front door.

"Where should we begin?" He followed me down the foot-path.

"The main road and light poles near traffic lights or tram and bus stops. Basically, where people stop the most has the best chance."

We walked side by side until we reached the main road, falling into an easy rhythm as we put up the posters. I held them against the poles while he secured them with tape, our movements synchronised without thought. As we worked, we made small talk—his favourite cafe on Main Road, the one with the best coffee, the little corner shop that sold food from the old country. Familiar comforts, pieces of home woven into the routine of our task.

"That's the last one." I returned the tape to my backpack as we finished.

"Great."

We were on his street, having hung up posters in a square on the streets around his house.

"Can I come in and go to the toilet before I leave?" I asked as we reached his front gate.

"Of course."

I followed him up the path, waiting as he unlocked the door and held it open for me. Stepping inside, I dropped my backpack in the living room before heading down the hall. In the bathroom, I lingered, catching my reflection in the mirror. The sun had flushed my cheeks, and my scalp was tinged red—a telltale sign of sunburn. I ran my fingers through my hair, then exhaled, unlocking the door and making my way back. Just as I'd hoped, he was settled in his armchair.

"Do you mind if I get some water?" I picked up my backpack and got out my water bottle. I scanned the shelf above the heater as I walked into the kitchen. He'd returned his keys to the bowl. I filled up my water bottle and returned, putting it in my backpack, before walking over to the photo.

"I hope we find you soon." I talked to the framed photo as my hand reached up and collected the keys in my fist. "Will you let me know if he returns?" I lifted my backpack over my shoulder, deftly sliding the keys into it as I did.

"I'll call you." Miroslav stood and walked me to the door. "Thank you for helping me."

I stepped out of the doorway. "Of course, anything for a fellow countryman." I smiled and walked jauntily down the street, the keys jostling in my backpack as I went. I waved, and Miroslav returned to his house.

I quickened my pace when his front door clicked shut, striding swiftly toward the main road. Time was critical—if this was going to work, I had to move fast. Pushing open the door of the small shoe repair shop, I stepped inside, slightly out of breath. "Can you make a copy of these keys now?" I asked, pulling Miroslav's keys from my pocket and placing them on the counter.

The man behind the counter took them and carefully checked all the keys against the template he had hanging on a rack. "I'll be 20 minutes."

"Okay, I'll wait." I sat on the chair by the door and picked up a magazine from the table beside it. I attempted reading, but my mind kept returning to Miroslav. My plan hinged on him not knowing that I'd taken his keys. For that to happen, I had to return them without his awareness. I was not looking forward to this next part. My leg began jiggling as nerves hit me. This was going to be hard.

After the longest twenty minutes of my life, the man finally called me over. I paid quickly, slipping Miroslav's keys into my left pocket and the copy into my right. Stepping outside, I turned left, taking the parallel street to Miroslav's. If I wanted to get inside without him noticing, I had to be careful—his armchair was perfectly positioned to watch the front of his house. I walked briskly, scanning house numbers until I found the one that matched Miroslav's. Stopping at the fence, I peered over into the backyard. Beyond it, I spotted his roof. I had my way in.

I kneeled, tied, and re-tied my shoe as I scoped out the house. It was a pale blue weatherboard with dark blue edging. The house was well maintained, with no cars in the front yard. Hopefully, it belonged to a DUNK—double income couple with no kids. The small gate to the driveway was open, and there was a garage at the back with no gate in between. I checked up and down the street. It was empty and quiet. No one was around. It was now or never. I stood from tying my shoes and walked down the driveway and into the backyard, which was full of fruit trees and a garden bed. Running to the back fence, I climbed up, vaulting into Miroslav's backyard, expecting someone to shout at any moment. I landed in the backyard and crouched down, waiting. No one shouted.

I crab-walked through Miroslav's backyard to the back door and listened. I could hear the television and nothing else. Crouching down, I walked around the corner to the window I had left open. I slowly pushed it open and climbed in, leaving my backpack on the ground. As I slithered inside over the sill, my skin prickled with nerves. The bedroom door was open; if Miroslav walked past, he would see me. I gently placed my feet on the floor and tiptoed to the bedroom door, listening. I heard snoring over the sound of the television. Relief flooded me. He was sleeping.

I tiptoed down the hallway and into the kitchen. Miroslav's feet on the armchair in front of me, his snoring now louder. I gently placed the keys on the kitchen table. It was too risky to go into the living room where he was and return them to the bowl. Hopefully, he'd assume he placed it there instead of the bowl and not think too much about it.

I tiptoed back down the hallway and was in the bedroom, halfway between the door and the window, when Miroslav screamed.

"Stop, don't do it," he shouted in our language. "I won't do it. I won't."

I froze, breaking out in sweat as I breathed shallowly. I eyed the window. If I ran and jumped out, he would hear me. My instinct told me to hide. I tiptoed behind the door and crouched down, waiting.

"Please leave me alone. I didn't want to do it." He pleaded, his voice guttural.

Who was he talking to? No one else was in the house, and the phone didn't ring.

He muttered under his breath, and then there was another deep sigh. The chair creaked, and I heard his footsteps down the hall. I watched him from the crack between the door and the wall as he walked to the end of the hallway and entered the bathroom. Thankfully, the door to the bedroom was before the bathroom. While he was occupied, I gently tiptoed to the window and jumped out, carefully sliding it shut. I went to his side gate and jumped over, before running through his front yard and onto the street. I didn't stop running until I was at the tram stop.

As I sat on the tram seat, I breathed out my relief. My plan had worked. Exhilaration buoyed me as I reached into my pocket and took out the spare keys. I now had a way of collecting information about Miroslav to prove he was involved in the genocide, to expose him. I wondered who he was talking to. He sounded tortured, but then again, all of us from the war carried our war wounds, and they seeped out while we were unconscious, in night terrors that returned us to the site of our own hell. My hand clenched on the keys. He deserved to suffer, and I would make sure he suffered more.

12-Intruder

I waited a week. By now, I knew Miroslav's shift schedule. On Tuesday, I stationed myself down the street, watching as he left for work. Then I waited an extra fifteen minutes—just to be sure. The urge to use the keys burned inside me, but I forced myself to be patient. I was too close to my goal to make a mistake now. When Miroslav didn't return, I started down the street, my heartbeat quickening. As I slipped the key into his front door lock, my shoulders tensed, bracing for someone to call out, to ask what I was doing. One final glance over my shoulder. Nothing. The street was still, the neighbours were inside or at work. I ducked in and shut the door behind me.

I locked the door and stood in the hallway, letting the silence settle in. Even though I had watched Miroslav walk to work, his presence was in the house. I walked into the living room, walking on the edges of the room so I wasn't visible to the outside. I thought about drawing the curtains, but that was so obviously out of character for Miroslav, and then if he returned early, he'd immediately know something was amiss, not to mention that I might forget to leave the house as it was and make him aware of my secret visit.

I went to the bedroom. That was usually where people kept things of note. There were sheer curtains over the windows, so I didn't have to worry about anyone seeing me. He had made the bed before he left for the day, covering it with a thick orange blanket of a tiger that he used as a bedspread.

There was an ashtray on the bedside table with a library book, a thriller in our language, on his side of the bed. I rifled through the drawer and found letters from his daughters to him, neatly bundled and well thumbed, with photos of them in front of main landmarks in Queensland, at a beach in one-piece swimsuits, in front of a ride at Dreamworld, on a rollercoaster, in their school uniforms.

I walked to the bedside table on the other side and opened the drawer. Inside was hand cream, panadol, and a crumpled piece of paper. I took it out, smoothed it, and sat on the bed in a rush as I read the first few words.

Dear Miroslav

I know I am taking the coward's way out in writing this, but it is too hard to speak to you. We came to Australia to get away from the hatred and vitriol in Serbia. This was supposed to be our new start. We were leaving our past behind and embracing our future.

And then you betrayed me and your daughters again at the wedding. I know you say you were drunk, that Branko provoked you with his taunts about Srebrenica. That his brother had told him how you were a traitor to Serbia when you told everyone about the massacre being real because you were there as a bus driver. And that may be true, but now it is me and your daughters who suffer.

We are the ones who cannot go among our community without being labelled the traitor's daughters, or the traitor's wife. We are the ones whose sleep is broken with bricks thrown through our window. We are the ones who are scorned and cast aside.

You keep telling me to be strong. To not let their words cow me, but I cannot. I just wanted a new life, a sense of purpose and belonging, but that is gone again.

All you had to do was keep your promise not to speak about Srebrenica. Not to share any of your experiences as a soldier, but you could not keep quiet, and so I cannot stay by your side. I cannot let my daughters suffer the wrath of our community as they take out their anger on us.

I am leaving you and taking the girls to Queensland. My sister has found us a house to rent and a job with her cleaning crew. I know it is cowardly and terrible to leave while you are at work and let you find out when you come home to an empty house, but I cannot talk to you anymore.

You will attempt to convince me to stay, or to let you come with us so we start fresh as a family, but I do not want that. I want to make a new life, leave the unpleasantness and hardship of war behind.

I will get the girls to write to you when we arrive, and you will have our address. When we get a phone, they can call you. One day, the girls can come and visit you, but for now, we need time to establish ourselves.

Gordana

This was the proof. The definitive proof he was at the genocide. If he was a bus driver, then he must have driven the women to the free territory and then the men and boys to the massacre.

I was trembling. This was the smoking gun I was looking for. Best of all, this meant that Alyssa could expose him with a newspaper article and not worry that it would send him scurrying to Serbia. He had escaped to Australia - there was no going back.

I rifled through his wardrobe. Found a box of documents. Among them his discharge papers from the Serbian army. They listed his dates of service. He was in transport. His bus career probably allowed him to transport soldiers and equipment.

I remembered being on the bus after we left Potočari. Ramo's mother screaming his name. A UN soldier was there to protect us and get us to safe territory. As we travelled for hours through Serb territory, there were villagers by the road, shouting and screaming. Some buses were turned off, others were stopped, and women were made to disembark. There were stories of women who had gone missing, never finding their way to the refugee camp, possibly taken to rape camps. Miroslav was one of the bus drivers. He was one of those who transported the women. Maybe he was driving one of the buses that veered off the road to the free territory. What other acts of horror had he committed? My stomach churned with nausea. He needed to pay for what he did.

I had to call Alyssa and give her all the information. She could finally publish. She could expose him. I still clutched the letter in my hand. What to do with it? If I took it with me, he would suspect someone was in the house. And even if I took it and gave it to Alyssa, how would that help her? She couldn't do anything with the letter.

I sat on the bed with a thud. I couldn't tell Alyssa about the letter. To do that would mean to implicate myself. Damnit, what could I do? How could I get the information to Alyssa confirming Miroslav's service and that he had talked about it?

There was no date on the letter to track down the wedding and a witness; even if I did, they wouldn't want to talk to me. If only there was someone I knew in the Serbian community that I could use as a witness. I looked up at the mirror on the wardrobe opposite me and caught sight of my blonde hair. An idea formed. I returned the letter to the dresser and wrote all the details on the service record in my notebook.

I went to the other bedrooms, poked through boxes, looking for more clues. In one box in the spare bedroom, I found a brick with the word traitor written on it. This was the brick that had been thrown in his window. It seemed macabre to keep it, but I could see myself doing the same. This brick signified the end of his life with his family. There was a certain heftiness to that. I returned the brick to the box.

I went into the kitchen. Opened the cupboards. There were cans of pašteta, chicken paste that we Yugos put on bread. Bags of soup from the home country. Cans of baked beans and spaghetti. In the small bar fridge were milk, butter, and eggs. He mustn't be much of a cook, or maybe it was really depressing to be just cooking for one. On the kitchen table were a phone and an electricity bill. I picked up the phone, dialled the phone company. When I asked, I gave them the account number on the bill. I confirmed the biller's name and gave Miroslav's date of birth, which I'd collected from his private papers.

"How can I help you?" the operator asked.

"I'm moving and would like to cancel my phone at the earliest opportunity." I returned the bill to the table with a smile.

"Would you like us to divert the number to your new house?"

"No, thank you."

"That will take effect immediately."

After I hung up, I called the electricity company and did the same, giggling as I imagined Miroslav returning home in a few days, only to find neither his phone nor the electricity working. He would never be able to figure out how it got cancelled.

After I was sure I had looked at everything I could, I went to the bedroom to scout out the street, to leave the house. There was a neighbour across the street pruning her garden. Probably safest to go the back way. I left through the back door, carefully locking it, then jumping over the fence.

When I reached the city, I debated whether or not to see Alyssa. It would be better if I didn't see her face-to-face. I got on the train to St Albans and let myself be lulled into a hypnotic state as the train swayed on the tracks. I made a little script on a sheet of paper and practised it, muttering under my breath. The woman sitting next to me gave me a side-look and moved seats. I probably looked slightly crazed talking to myself. I felt it. I had to keep breathing in and out to calm myself so I could implement my plan.

I slipped into a phone box near my house, shielding myself from prying ears. My mother and Emir couldn't hear this conversation. With trembling hands, I dialled Alyssa's number, fumbling and having to start over more than once. My breath was unsteady, my pulse hammering in my ears. Finally, the line began to ring.

"I have news," I told her, my voice slightly shaky.

"What is it? What happened?" she asked.

"He admitted it. He admitted he was in Srebrenica."

"Who did?" she asked.

"Miroslav. He admitted it."

"How do you know?"

"I was on the bus he was driving. These two women were talking to him in our language, and he said he was in Srebrenica." I'd thought about what to do. I had to avoid telling Alyssa about my covert identity. Once she knew the truth, she could interfere, stop me, and I couldn't allow that to happen.

"Okay, tell me what he said."

I told her about the bus.

"So he just told you he was there."

"Yes, we have him."

"We need more. We need dates, names, places of burial. We need hard facts that can be corroborated."

"What if we do a sting, like they do on cop shows? Where you put a microphone on me and I go undercover?"

"That's not a good idea. You're a civilian, and stings only work when the police are involved. Otherwise, you're just walking into a dangerous situation. You need to be patient. I've been digging into him, piecing together his story. I'm close to finding another witness to corroborate your account. I already have proof that he came to Australia after the massacre. Once I secure that corroboration, I can publish the story. That'll put enough pressure on the authorities to issue an arrest warrant and take him into custody."

"You said a month ago you were getting a witness. But still there's no one."

"These things take time, Seka. A story like this is not easy to get. We need to work slowly and carefully."

"I've waited and waited. I've waited for years, and nothing has happened, and you're just another person telling me to wait. I've had enough." Frustration surged through me, and I slammed my palm onto the glass, the sharp crack echoing through the room.

"Seka, please don't do something stupid. I need you to take care of yourself. You're a witness. You will need to testify at The Hague to get justice."

"And what will happen then?" I demanded, my voice rising with each word.

"He'll get sent to jail."

I promised I would wait. I had waited this long; surely, it was worth waiting for justice. But as I hung up the phone, uncertainty gnawed at me. My blood was singing with urgency and anger. I longed to uncover the truth, to make him pay for his crimes. Alyssa was wrong. I could get him to talk under the right circumstances and knew precisely what those would be.

13-Nightclub

Phuong-Vy and I were dancing while Tom went to the bar. Ninu was on a hunting trip with his cousins, and when Phuong-Vy invited me to go clubbing, I was at a loose end. A Mc-Hammer-Wannabe in white harem pants and a white singlet interjected himself between us. I started my aerobics moves to keep him at a distance. He crowded Phuong-Vy, who was too polite to make a scene. She hunched into herself, her body language screaming for him to fuck off, but McWannabe wasn't taking the hint.

"I have a boyfriend," Phuong-Vy said.

McWannabee pretended not to hear so he could get closer to her, his face close to hers. He pecked her on the cheek and laughed, thinking he was being oh, so cute.

"Tom," Phuong-Vy said, and I looked over my shoulder. Tom was upon us.

"Is this piss-ant bothering you?" He crowded McWannabe.

McWannabe jutted his chin out and the two of them lined up their dicks almost pressing against each other, as they dead-eyed.

"This is so stupid," I muttered.

Phuong-Vy reached for Tom's hand. "Come on, hun. Let's have a good night."

"Do you want to take this outside?" McWannabe said.

Tom smiled, delighted. "I'd fucking love to, mate." He put his arm around Phuong-Vy's shoulders and headed outside.

"Go through the back." I nodded to the back entrance for McWannabe.

"Nah, I can take that weak shit." He jutted out his chest more.

"Seriously, dickhead, just fuck off home." I stood in front of him, not letting him move.

"Don't tell me what to do, bitch."

I smiled and stepped aside. "Your funeral fucker."

I followed slowly. I had seen more than enough blood and carnage in my lifetime and was not looking forward to seeing more.

"Seka, we have to stop him." Phuong-Vy held my arm, her voice shrill with panic. "Please."

"I tried. I told McWannabe to fuck off home, but he won't listen."

"Talk to Tom."

"Seriously." I sighed and headed to the huddle forming in the alley to my left.

I was walking out of the club when I saw a familiar shadow. Looking closer, I realised that yes, it was my brother Emir. I moved to the side and stood behind a tall Islander boy, shadowing Emir as he walked through the lobby and into the club.

What the fuck was he doing here? I went back in and stood at the back wall, watching him. He went to the bar and got a shot, sipping it as he scoped the club, his eyes lingering on girls. I melted back into the shadows, and his eyes glanced over me. I saw him eyeing a brunette in a blue, shimmery dress. He approached, and they exchanged a few remarks, then Emir went to the bar. That hypocritical fuck. Always lecturing me about being Muslim and not drinking, yet here he was, doing the exact same shit.

I stepped forward to confront him, then thought better of it. A little ammunition was a good thing. I returned to the lobby and outside while his back was turned to the bar.

As I entered the lobby, I saw Tom with his mates and approached. "You need to stop this."

"What?" He posted, jutting his chest out. "That dog came onto my girlfriend."

"Yeah, and nothing happened. But you doing this is going to hurt Phuong-Vy. She doesn't deal well with violence."

"She'll be fine." He shooed me away as if he were shooing a fly. "People need to know that I take care of what's mine."

Phuong-Vy was standing behind him, her eyes blank.

"Don't worry, babe, I'll just teach him a lesson." Tom pushed her hair away from her face. She didn't respond, but he seemed unperturbed. "Here. Mind my backpack." He handed her a backpack and walked away.

I saw him join the mob in the alley as he and his mates left. "Let's go." I put my hand around her shoulders and steered her toward Flinders Street Station. A few minutes later, I heard shouts and screams, calls for police, and then stampeding footsteps. Tom ran past, his eyes glowing crazily, as he screamed in exhilaration. His crew ran with him, the three other thug boys who followed him everywhere.

"Meet you in our usual," Tom shouted as he ran past.

"Fuck him. We're going home," I told her.

"I have to return this." She touched the backpack on her shoulder.

"Fine. We give it back and then we fuck off."

She nodded, wiping tears from her eyes. "Do you think the guy is okay?"

"I'm sure he's fine," I lied. "They didn't have time to do much damage."

We walked into Bourke Street Mall and down the escalators to Hungry Jack's. This was our usual end-of-night stop. Tom and his crew were at a table, their voices loud, their gestures manic as they regaled each other with their tales of violence.

"He was bleeding from every orifice when we were done with him," Tom said gleefully.

"Yeah, I stomped that motherfucker good," Cueball next to him said. He was bald, and his shiny, long head was like a cue ball.

"There she is," Tom called out as I walked over. They were at our usual table at the back. "What took you so long?"

"I only run if there's a bomb," I said.

Tom guffawed loudly. He knew my history as a war refugee and was always impressed by how I wasn't phased by violence.

"Here." I took the backpack off her and handed it to him.

He looked behind me, his eyes widening. "Go to the toilets." He moved away from us and headed to the napkin dispenser. I looked behind and saw two police officers coming down the escalators.

I grabbed Phuong-Vy's hand and yanked her to the toilet. She saw the police officers and followed without a word.

When we got to the toilet, she went into the cubicle and threw up while I held her hair.

"It's my fault," she muttered. "It's all my fault."

I helped her up and put the toilet seat down, so she could sit. I rifled through my handbag and found my mints. I'd learned to always have them handy and gave her one.

"Thank you."

"It's not your fault. It's Tom's. He's not a good guy," I told her.

"Yeah, I know." Phuong-Vy sighed. "I thought I loved him."

Her talking in the past tense was a good sign. He was on the way out.

"I guess we'll have to find a new club, though."

Phuong-Vy pouted. "Fuck, yeah. He's going to get Metro in the breakup."

She went to the mirror and used water to wash out her face. "I look like dog shit," she said.

I picked up the backpack and carried it, placing it on the vanity against the wall. "What the fuck has he got in here?" My skin broke out in goose pimples as I remembered Tom's panicked look when the police came, the way he let her keep the backpack. Fuck.

I undid the zip.

"What are you doing?" she asked.

"I have a bad feeling." I rummaged through the bag, my fingers brushing against something cold and solid. My breath hitched as I peered inside. A black handle. "What the fuck is that?"Heart pounding, I reached in and pulled out the gun.

She gasped and stepped back, her eyes wide with panic. I carefully returned the gun to the backpack. I took out a tattered pencil case.

Before opening it, I knew what I would find—little bags of white powder.

Phuong-Vy's eyes opened wide with shock. "I didn't know, Seka. I promise, I didn't know."

"That fucking scum. I know you didn't. We're ending this shit now."

I picked up her backpack, put the gun in mine, and took the pencil case. "We're giving him his shit back and getting the fuck out of here."

Phuong-Vy opened the bathroom door and froze. She turned around, her eyes wide with horror. "Get rid of it," she whispered, taking my backpack.

I peered over her shoulder and saw the police had swarmed around Tom and his thugs, a melee breaking out.

A police officer saw Phuong-Vy and urged her out. Phuong-Vy closed the door in my face. I ran to the toilet cubicle, tipped out all the powder and flushed it. I hid the gun with damp paper towels in the rubbish bin and waited.

No one came in. After 10 minutes, I opened the door and peered out. The restaurant was empty. They were all gone. I went to leave, but couldn't. I returned, took the gun from the paper towel dispenser, and put it in my handbag, throwing away all my other belongings.

I called Phuong-Vy on her mobile, but there was no answer. I went to the counter. "What happened to my friend Phuong-Vy? She's Asian, has long black hair, and is wearing a white dress."

"Yeah, the police collected her and the rest of those thugs. They took them to the police station."

"Which one?" I asked.

"Bourke Street."

I climbed the escalators, feeling flustered and utterly out of sorts. My heart raced as I clutched my handbag closer, its weight a constant reminder of the dangerous secret it concealed. I couldn't possibly walk into the police station while carrying a gun. Logic dictated that I should dispose of it immediately, but something held me back. It was as if my long-harboured dreams of revenge were finally material-ising. Countless nights, I had spent fantasising about killing Miroslav, yet I never had the means. Now, in my possession was a gun that no one else knew about—a hidden power I was reluctant to relinquish. Yet, the dilemma gnawed at me; I couldn't abandon Phuong-Vy or return home to keep the gun safely tucked away. I needed a discreet place to store it, somewhere I could access easily when the time came.

I remembered the first time I saw Emir at Metro. He must have driven there, the only logical conclusion, given that he was the designated driver because he owned a car. I carried a spare key to his vehicle on my keychain. All I needed was to locate it amidst the jumble of keys. Phuong-Vy would wait. I walked briskly towards the nightclub. The nearest garage, the one everyone avoided due to its sky-high fees, was not his choice. Emir would never park there, opting instead for something more economical. I closed my eyes briefly, sifting through memories, trying to recall any mention he might have made. There was something about the Rialto, a towering high-rise with a bustling food court in its foyer. That was it. I navigated my way to the other end of Russell Street, my steps echoing in the quiet, and descended into the first level of the basement parking. The dimly lit space revealed no sign of his battered yellow Mazda hatchback. My search continued to the second level, where I finally found it in a corner. I opened the boot and lifted the edge of the carpet, revealing a small cavity, perhaps once meant for a spare part, now empty. Carefully, I wrapped the gun in one of Emir's old t-shirts, and tucked it inside the hollow. I meticulously replaced the carpet, smoothing it back to its original position and arranging items on top to disguise any disturbance. It was a perfect ruse; no one would suspect a thing. With a final glance around, I locked the car and began my ascent up the stairs. Suddenly, the sound of male voices, speaking in Bosnian, reached my ears. Instinctively, I ducked behind one of the sturdy pillars, my heart racing. From my concealment, I watched as Emir and his friends approached and casually got into the car, their laughter and conversation punctuating the silence of the garage.

As they drove away, my stress levels lowered. It was safe. The gun was safe. Now I needed to find Phuong-Vy.

By the time I staggered into the police station, my skin glistened with perspiration, and my cheeks were flushed from the night's heat. I approached the front desk and asked for Phuong-Vy. The officer told me she would be leaving shortly. I sat in the sterile waiting room waited. Moments later, the door opened and out stepped Phuong-Vy, her tired eyes were rimmed with red from a night without sleep. A female officer accompanied her. Her makeup was smeared away, revealing a raw vulnerability beneath the hardened exterior, making her look so young and innocent.

"What happened?" I asked.

The officer replied in a measured tone, "Your friend has had quite the night. No charges were pressed against her, but we did need a detailed witness statement. Take my card and call me if you need anything further." She extended a business card.

Gently, I led Phuong-Vy out of the precinct, the cool night air washing over us as we stepped onto the city sidewalks. "We'll catch a taxi home," I declared, guiding her toward the familiar corner. This ride was a rare indulgence, one we had savoured only once before on my birthday. Normally, we would take the NightRider bus—a free service.

I flagged down a taxi on the rain-slicked street, and we sank into the back seat. Upon arriving at her bungalow, she darted off to jump in the shower. Soon enough, she emerged clad in comfortable pyjamas, and I changed into my own.

The aroma of brewing hot chocolate soon filled the small kitchen as I warmed milk on her stove. Settling across from each other at the worn wooden table, I gently asked again, "So what happened?"

"The boy that Tom beat up ended up in the hospital with a head injury. He's in a critical condition; they say he might not make it. The police officer mentioned that if he dies, Tom could face charges of manslaughter."

"Fuck. Well, he had it coming," I muttered. "We both tried to talk him out of it."

She paused, sipping her milk. "What did you do with the stuff in his backpack?"

"I poured the powder down the sink and then made my way to the Yarra River. I had to walk down to the secluded bank where no one could see me, and I threw it into the current. I needed to be certain that nothing was left behind, which is why it took me so long to meet you."

Her voice trembled with relief. "I'm glad. I want this whole chapter out of my life. I want Tom gone from my life for good."

"We'll make that happen," I vowed.

Later, as I drifted off to sleep, vivid images danced before my eyes—Miroslav on his knees while I held a cold, unyielding gun to his head, forcing him to confess. The intoxicating rush of power reminded me that I was now in control, and he would, in time, submit to my will.

We were jolted awake by a loud pounding on the door, echoing through the quiet of the morning. I trailed behind Phuong-Vy, my heart pounding as I saw Tom standing there, looking dishevelled. "Hey, babe. How are you?" he greeted, his voice smooth but with an edge of desperation.

"Why aren't you in jail?" I shot back.

"I have to appear on summons. I'm out until I have to go to court," he explained, his eyes darting nervously.

He attempted to push his way in, but Phuong-Vy stood firm, the strength in her small frame keeping the door resolutely closed. "You're not coming in."

"Come on babe, it was a misunderstanding," he pleaded, his smile laced with charm that failed to reach his eyes. She remained unmoved.

I positioned myself behind her. "Fuck off. You're not wanted here," I growled.

"Okay, okay," he muttered, his facade of charm slipping away to reveal a reptilian glint in his eyes. "Look, I'm just here for your gear."

"Are you for real?" I shouted, my voice rising with disbelief. "We could have been arrested because of you. I flushed that shit down the toilet."

"Fuck, fuck," he muttered, panic flickering across his face. "Are you sure it's not here?" He craned his neck, peering into the dim interior of the bungalow.

"It's not here. It's in the plumbing at Hungry Jacks," I replied with a tone of finality.

"What about the other thing?" he pressed, desperate.

"The other thing. You mean the gun, right?" Phuong-Vy asked, her voice steady and cold. He nodded quickly, biting his thumbnail nervously. "Seka threw it in the Yarra River," she added.

"Fuck, you've got to be kidding me." His frustration erupted as he punched the wall beside the door, the thud resonating through the air. "That was my grandfather's revolver from WWII. My father's going to kill me if he realises I took it." He rubbed the back of his neck, twitching with anxiety.

"What the fuck did you think I was going to do? Walk into the police station carrying an illegal gun and a backpack that had drugs in it? No wonder you were arrested, dickhead!" I retorted, my voice dripping with exasperation and fury.

His face contorted with rage, dark shadows playing across his features as he stepped toward the door. But Phuong-Vy was quicker, slamming it shut in his face. "Go away or I'll call the police," she shouted through the barrier as she turned the lock. "And I'm breaking up with you," she added. We waited with bated breath by the door, straining to hear any sound beyond the silence that enveloped us. We tiptoed cautiously into the living room, careful not to make a noise and peered through the narrow slats of the blinds. There he stood, a brooding figure in the dim light.

"Come on, babe, don't be like this," Tom called out when he noticed the blinds lift slightly.

"I'm not joking, Tom. We're done. I never want to see you again. If you come here, I'll call the police," she declared letting the blind fall back into place. We retreated from the window.

"Fuck you, bitch," Tom spat venomously. His fists pounded the door several times, each thud echoing ominously. "You fucking cocktease."

She pressed a finger to her lips, signalling me to stay quiet. We stood there, our breaths shallow, listening intently until the sound of stomping footsteps faded into the distance. We waited several more heart-stopping moments before she cautiously raised the blind again. Her backyard lay empty. "He's gone," she whispered with palpable relief.

"Good riddance to bad rubbish," I muttered with a sense of finality.

"I know," she agreed, as she sank onto the couch, clutching a cushion tightly. "I wish I'd never met him."

I joined her, sitting close and wrapping my arms around her, our heads naturally tilting toward each other for comfort. "I'm sorry he hurt you," I murmured, my hand rubbing her arm in a soothing gesture. I could never confess that I didn't share her wish, yet my mind was already racing ahead, contemplating the possibilities that now lay before me. Without Tom, none of this would have been possible, and the thought of the gun in Emir's car loomed large in my mind.

14-Target

I was working when I saw Ninu parking his Ranger truck through the glass doors. I ran through the reception area and hugged him as he got out of the truck.

"That's not the welcome I was expecting." He hugged me back, kissing the top of my head.

"I missed you." I smiled, looking up at him. It was a beautiful sunny day full of possibilities. Revenge and retribution fantasies loomed large in my mind.

"I missed you too," he said, his face lit up with a smile.

"How was your weekend away?"

"Great."

"Did you hunt anything?"

Ninu shrugged. "My cousins tried, but their aim is for shit. We mostly just drove around the bush shooting trees." He put his arm around my shoulders and we walked back into the vet clinic. "It's not as much fun as it used to be."

"Maybe you don't have the right company." I smiled suggestively.

"You want to go hunting?" Ninu asked, looking at me with surprise.

"Well, I want to do the shooting part. The hunting, not so much."

"Maybe we could camp overnight?" Ninu was enthusiastic.

My only experience with camping was when my family had to hide in the forest when the Serbs attacked Srebrenica. We'd spent three weeks living in a tent without running water or plumbing.

"I'd love to," I lied. I needed to achieve my plan, and for that, I needed to learn how to use the gun that was now hidden in my shed at home.

"Great. Let's go camping this weekend." He kissed me on the lips.

That Saturday morning, I found myself waiting for Ninu on a deserted back street near the university. I had arranged for him to pick me up far from the probing eyes of my family and the ever-watchful Bosnians. Soon enough, his red ute rattled up the road, its engine purring as it pulled to a stop. I eased open the passenger door and slid into the worn leather seat.

"Hi," he murmured as he leaned over, planting a searing kiss on my lips. His kiss was hot and insistent, igniting a spark of rebellion within me.

"Hello yourself," I replied, returning his fervour with my own kiss. A surge of adrenaline flooded my veins as I revelled in the unfolding of my secret plan. Ninu turned the key in the ignition and stepped on the accelerator, the ute shuddering to life as we merged onto the road. The tuned radio softly hummed in the background, and Ninu began to sing, his voice mingling with the engine's hum. "How's vet school treating you?" he asked.

"Okay," I replied, though the single word belied my deep malaise. I felt like I was sleepwalking through my life, detached and listless. He was the only person who allowed me to drop my defences, to momentarily be vulnerable. "Boring as bat shit," I added, reaching for a cigarette. The flame flickered as I lit it, the smoke weaving into the cool night air.

For nearly 45 minutes, we sped out of the city limits, venturing deep into the quiet embrace of a country town. The dirt roads wound sinuously through vast tracts of land, the car's tires sending plumes of dust into the air. I looked out the window, witnessing how the dust danced in the glow of the streetlights, each shaft of light turning the airborne particles into glittering motes.

"Where are we?" I asked, the question almost lost in the rhythmic hum of the road and the rustling of the wind over the open fields.

"Kyneton," he answered. "There's some good scrub coming up that the wild pigs love."

As Ninu continued driving deeper into the rural expanse, the terrain transformed. The woods grew denser and more unpredictable, their branches clawing at the sky. I couldn't help but marvel at how this landscape diverged from the memories of Srebrenica, where I grew up—the trees here appeared stunted, their trunks a patchwork of browns and greys, as if the relentless sun had mercilessly drained all the colour and life from their bark. Eventually, Ninu turned down a narrow dirt road that seemed to close in around the vehicle. He brought the ute to a stop, its engine sputtering to silence. "We have to walk from here," he announced.

Stepping out into the sweltering heat, I trailed after him to the back of the ute. The sticky warmth of the day clung to my skin, and a sheen of perspiration glistened along my back. Ninu handed me a well-worn sleeping bag and a rugged duffel bag, before hoisting an esky and additional supplies onto his shoulder. We walked in silence for several hundred metres along a narrow, winding track, the gentle roar of a nearby river steadily growing louder, promising respite.Eventually, we emerged from the track into a clearing that revealed a sandy beach along the edge of a slowly meandering, brown river. The area was encircled by trees that offered dappled shade, and the sudden coolness brought a sigh of relief as the temperature seemed to dip beneath the oppressive heat.

"My dad's friend owns this land," Ninu explained, carefully stacking the bags in a corner. "He lets us camp here." Without a moment's hesitation, he grinned. "Let's go for a swim." With that, he peeled off his shirt and untucked his shoes.

"I didn't bring my swimsuit," I admitted.

"Neither did I," he replied with a roguish smile. In one swift, daring motion, Ninu yanked down his shorts, discarding them along with his underwear. There he stood, unabashedly naked in the glare of broad daylight.

"What are you doing? Someone will see you!" I muttered, glancing frantically around the secluded clearing.

"No one comes here. We're completely alone," he assured me with a conspiratorial glint in his eye. Tenderly, he reached for my t-shirt and pulled it over my head, revealing skin that seemed to glow under the filtered light. With one final, cautious look around the shadowed clearing, I relinquished my inhibitions and followed suit, shedding my clothes until we were both as bare as nature intended. Carefully, we left our belongings in a neat pile before dashing into the inviting water.

The shock of the cold river against our heated skin was electrifying, a bracing contrast that sent shivers and tingles running through us. We frolicked playfully at first, our laughter mingling with the sound of the flowing water, our games gradually morphing into a tender foreplay. In the intimacy of the river, Ninu carried me effortlessly to the sandy bank where, with passion kindled under the watchful canopy of trees, we made love. Afterwards, we returned to the river, letting its gentle current wash away the remnants of our heat and abandon. The water embraced us like a healing balm.

"Now let's shoot," I announced with a mischievous glint in my eye as I pulled on my t-shirt, deliberately leaving my bra untouched—after all, there was no one around to see me. The cool air brushed against my bare skin, and I could feel the fine fabric cling comfortably to every contour of my body.

Ninu's gaze dropped to my exposed, puckered nipples, accentuated by the damp material. As his hand reached toward me, I quickly slapped it away, my pulse quickening with playful defiance.

"Shooting now. Play later," I declared, voice ringing with authority.

"Yes, ma'am," he replied, his tone light as he gave a playful salute. He slipped into his shorts, purposely leaving his strong torso bare, his skin bathed in the dappled sunlight that filtered through the trees. Digging through the duffel bag I'd carried, he selected a rifle and handgun with a casual precision.

While he focused on gathering his gear, I stealthily retrieved my secret artefact and slipped it into my pocket.

Ninu smoothly handed me the handgun before slinging the rifle over his shoulder. "I've got ammunition here," he explained, rummaging briefly to produce two boxes, which he tucked securely into his pocket.

I cradled the handgun gingerly in my hand, every touch sending small sparks of apprehension. "Don't worry, it isn't loaded," Ninu observed, noting my cautious grip with an amused undertone.

He walked confidently down the narrow dirt path that led back to the truck before emerging onto the other side. We found ourselves in a secluded clearing, a natural arena encircled by towering trees whose leaves danced with shimmering sunlight. Ahead, the forest floor dipped into a gentle indentation, and a solitary tree stood before us with a bold red circle drawn on its trunk. Drawing closer, I noticed the bark was rough and pockmarked.

"That's our target. What do you want to start with?"

I raised the gun slightly as an unspoken declaration, prompting Ninu to lean his rifle against a sturdy tree to our left. Taking the handgun from me, he carefully lifted its mechanism, methodically preparing to unlock the barrel.

"How did you do that?" I asked, my eyes narrowing as I inspected the handgun. My mind raced back to the countless tries with Tom's gun—nights filled with sweat-drenched anxiety and desperate squirming, praying not to set off an unexpected explosion. Eventually, after hours immersed in research and poring over a detailed manual on a gun manufacturing site, I'd managed to unlock the barrel of my Smith

& Wesson Victory Model revolver—a piece with its roots in WWII. Each successful manoeuvre had come more from luck than refined technique. After a mass shooting in 1996, the government initiated an amnesty program where firearms were surrendered to police to be destroyed. Possessing an illegal firearm meant risking jail, so I was forced to keep it hidden.

"Here," Ninu said, demonstrating slowly and deliberately, his hands tracing a careful, step-by-step process. He repeated the action a second time to emphasise his point. "Now do you want to try?" he inquired as he passed me the unloaded handgun.

I practised before his observant eyes; his occasional gentle intervention and supportive nods encouraged persistence until, with trembling determination, I finally managed to open the barrel without incident.

"I'll show you how to put the bullets in," he said.

I extended the handgun to him exactly as he had demonstrated—held securely away from my body, muzzle pointed downward. In response, he took it, his hands steady as he opened the chamber to insert the bullets. Carefully closing the barrel, he returned the handgun to me. I mirrored his movements exactly, slotting the bullets in with deliberate caution and precision.

"Now it's time to practice," he declared, retrieving the gun from me and stepping back to model the perfect shooting posture. "When you press the trigger, there will be recoil—it'll feel like your hand is jolted, but you must maintain your grip. And be prepared for the deafening sound."

I chuckled darkly, "I know how loud ammunition can be," my tone imbued with memories of a three-year siege and the barrage of thunderous rounds. Over time, I had come to discern the guttural boom of a tank shell from the staccato bursts of a machine gun.

"Sorry," Ninu said with a sheepish grin, his eyes crinkling in camaraderie. "When shooting, you need to stand with your feet firmly apart, knees flexed, and both arms outstretched while cradling the gun." He modelled the stance perfectly. "Then, take a deep breath and shoot." With that, he pressed the trigger; the muzzle jolted, and the explosive bang resonated through the clearing, momentarily startling me despite my anticipation.

"Your turn," Ninu announced, passing the handgun back to me.

I mimicked his stance with earnest concentration, his presence behind me guiding every adjustment. He lingered a bit too long close by until I shot him a warning look, prompting him to step back hastily. My initial attempts were wild; each trigger pull sent the bullet careening off the intended mark, the shots missing the tree entirely.

"Good. You're getting the hang of it," Ninu encouraged playfully.

"Don't patronise me," I retorted, a spark of defiant humour in my voice.

Ninu's smile broadened as he held the ammunition box with a sense of shared triumph. I opened the barrel again, carefully replenishing it with bullets before snapping it shut and re-establishing the precise shooter's stance that Ninu had so patiently modelled.

As I steadied myself, thoughts of Tom's resolute face and memories of Miroslav steeled my hand. I aimed squarely at the tree and fired—a perfect, determined shot that struck true. The satisfying thud of the bullet embedding itself in the bark confirmed my success.

"Wow, you got it," Ninu cheered as he inspected the bullet marks with delight.

A surge of exhilaration radiated through me. I fired several more rounds, each a testament to my growing confidence, before Ninu signalled it was his turn again.

"Do you want to try the rifle?" he asked.

I shook my head, content with my progress and the harmony of the moment. I watched intently as Ninu handled the rifle with the precision of a master marksman, each shot striking the bullseye with unwavering accuracy.

"Okay, let's pack it up for the day," he eventually said, his tone carrying both satisfaction and a hint of fatigue. As he strolled over to the target tree, he gathered the spent casings that lay scattered, methodically placing them into the empty ammunition box. I bent down, retrieving a stray bullet I'd secretly taken from Tom's gun, and feigned discovery as I handed it back to him.

"This one looks different," I remarked, holding out the intact bullet.

"I must have dropped it," he replied with an amused shrug, tucking it away in the ammunition box from which he'd been extracting bullets earlier.

By the end of the camping trip, seizing that box of ammunition would mean my plan had succeeded.

Later that night, we settled in for the night, under a vast, starlit sky and on a sandy beach that glowed in the pale lunar light. Ninu unzipped both sleeping bags and melded them together. Skin pressed against skin, we shared the raw intimacy of the night. Multiple bouts of passion ensued before I finally lay back, cradled in his strong arms, the rhythmic sound of the river serenading us. In that perfect, tender silence, I realised I could get used to this.

"When will I meet your family?" he asked, stroking my hair. I stiffened.

"What's wrong?" he asked as I moved away from him.

"My mother and brother won't approve of us dating. In fact, they might disown me if they knew I was dating you." My voice wavered slightly, the fire's glow flickering across his suddenly worried expression.

"Really?" He sat up, drawing his knees to his chest, the flames casting dancing shadows on his face. "But we're Australian."

"They're Muslim, and we've just survived a war where we were being killed for our religious beliefs. They won't accept us." My words hung heavy in the crisp night air, punctuated by the crackling of burning wood.

"So we're going to keep it a secret forever, or until we get sick of hiding." His tone was resigned, yet a hint of defiance lingered.

"No, that's not what I'm saying." I reached for him, wrapping my arms around him, feeling the warmth of his bare skin against mine. Fear surged through me at the thought of him growing weary of us. I hadn't realised how deeply I wanted to be with him until I faced the possibility of being without him. "They might just need some time to come around. I mean, it's not like your parents are overjoyed."

"My parents don't care. They only want me to be happy." His voice softened, the reassurance in his words wrapping around me like a comforting blanket.

"But didn't your mother insist that your niece get christened, even though your brother in law didn't want it?" I asked, remembering when he'd told me the story about his Catholic story marrying her Protestant husband.

"That's just an empty tradition. It doesn't mean anything." He shrugged, dismissing it with a casual wave of his hand.

"But it will mean something. I don't know if I want children, and if I do, I know I don't want them to be indoctrinated into any religion."

"Then they won't. We don't need to conform to any of the bullshit we don't believe in. We just have to love each other and be happy. I love you, Seka. I want to be with you. Not like a secret or something you're ashamed of. I want to be completely yours, and I want you to be completely mine." His words were a vow, as steady as the earth beneath us.

"I want that too." The sincerity in my voice echoed in the quiet night. We kissed, sealing our whispered promises beneath the vast, star-studded sky.

"But I think I might lose my family if they find out about us."

"Then we won't tell them anything. We'll just enjoy what we have for today." He hugged me tighter.

The next day, we packed up, the morning sun casting long shadows as Ninu drove us back to the suburbs and the routine of my regular life. I watched the bush retreat behind us, a sense of regret mingling with the dusty remnants of our getaway, as the wild beauty of the landscape faded into the distance.

15-Corpse

I drove Ninu's truck slowly down the quiet streets toward Miroslav's house, my headlights cutting through the early evening gloom. It was 5 pm, and as I passed by, I could see that the living room was warmly lit, the window invitingly open to the cool air. Inside, Miroslav was on the couch with the television casting flickering shadows across his face. A reluctant satisfaction stirred within me at seeing his pained expression.

Turning two blocks from his house, I pulled up at the local vet's car park. I left the truck running, the engine purring softly in the background, and hoisted the lifeless carcass over my shoulder. I could feel the heavy, unpleasant weight of dry, flopping body parts as I carried the remains to the front door.

The dog had been in my freezer for a week. Earlier, I'd called the real owners and paid for a cemetery plot and headstone for their Snookie. They had somewhere to grieve now—even if the grave was empty. Miroslav wouldn't know the difference. To him, Lux would have died in an accident.

Earlier that day, I had retrieved the thawed, dead German Shepherd from the freezer, noting that Miroslav wouldn't be able to tell the difference. In his mind, Lux would appear to have suffered a tragic accident. I drove to his local vet clinic. "Some guy just hit this dog with his car," I grunted as I hefted the body inside.

The receptionist gestured me into the back room. I gently set the dog onto the surgery table as she lightly touched its neck. "It's dead," she said.

"Oh, wow. I thought it was still alive," I said, as I pretended to wipe a tear from my cheek.

She told me she'd check for a microchip to notify the owner. "Okay," I replied, stepping backward toward the door before returning to the truck and driving around the block.

I expected a rapid two-minute check for the microchip and another two minutes for a follow-up call. Passing Miroslav's house again, I paused at the top of the street and watched his driveway in the rearview mirror. I noticed his car backing out. I followed him to the vet and parked my truck on the street, facing the double doors that led to the reception area.

I waited, knowing full well that this was the most crucial part of my plan. Devoted owners often knew every quirk and detail about their dogs, and there was a small possibility that Miroslav might deny the grim reality that the dog before him was indeed his pet. This was precisely where I hoped the undeniable evidence of the microchip would tip the scales in my favour. In his heart, having spent an entire week missing his dog, he half expected a phone call. It was this hope, coupled with the stark, clinical truth of the microchip, that I was banking on.

The door creaked open, and Miroslav emerged, cradling what appeared to be the lifeless body of a dog, wrapped tightly in plastic. Trailing behind him, the receptionist moved briskly to his car, the keys jingling as she unlocked the boot. Miroslav, however, shook his head, his expression a silent plea. She acknowledged his unspoken request, closing the boot and instead opening the back door. Miroslav bent down, gently placing his deceased pet inside.

The receptionist handed him the keys, and as he turned toward me, the transformation in his demeanour was undeniable. Grief had hollowed him out. His face looked older, drained. I felt a grim satisfaction quickly followed by guilt—and then reminded myself Miroslav was not human. He was a monster, a war criminal masquerading as an innocent man.

I navigated the streets ahead of him, returning to his house and parking at the top of the street. As he drove past, I ducked down. Once he pulled into the driveway, I emerged and walked by, aware of the risk but driven by an insatiable need to see more. My disguise was flawless; Ninu's work gear—a pair of black pants and a high-vis vest—transformed my appearance. My hair, tucked beneath a cap, ensured I was unrecognisable. As I strolled past his house, the rhythmic thud of a shovel piercing the earth reached my ears, punctuated by the soft, heartbreaking sounds of stifled sobs. Over the side gate, I glimpsed Miroslav's hunched figure, his shoulders and head visible as he dug a grave. The scene was almost poetic in its perfection. With a newfound spring in my step, I circled the block and returned to Ninu's truck. The next phase of my plan was ready to unfold.

At work the following day, I dialled his phone number with a mix of anticipation and satisfaction. When he answered, my voice was upbeat and cheerful. "My friend at the shelter called to say a German Shepherd was picked up without a microchip. Maybe it's Lux. I can give you the information."

"It's not Lux." His voice was weary and resigned. "Lux is dead."

"Oh no, I'm so sorry." I gasped. "How did it happen?"

"He was hit by a car. My local vet clinic called me."

"I'm so sorry for your loss."

"Thank you."

Our conversation ended shortly after.

The following day, I walked down Miroslav's street, clad in my favourite pair of jeans and a simple t-shirt, a basket clutched tightly in my hands. My heart was a mix of excitement and anxiety. This plan needed to work, but if it didn't, I had my backup plan. I had the gun. I had taken it from Emir's boot and concealed it in the shed in our backyard, hidden in a box under the bottom shelf amidst knick-knacks, until today when I transferred it to my backpack.

I lifted my backpack slightly, slipping my hand inside to clutch the handle of the gun briefly, feeling a rush of adrenaline and a sense of security as I imagined drawing it, aiming it at him. No, that was strictly a precautionary measure.

I approached his door and gently placed the basket on the doorstep. As I turned to leave, the front door creaked open behind me, and Miroslav called my name.

I turned, feigning surprise. "I thought you were at work. I was just dropping off a gift basket to express my condolences."

He opened the flyscreen door and stepped out, picking up the basket, scrutinising its contents. I had filled it with items from my local Yugo shop, all reminiscent of our homeland.

The pašteta he favoured, hearty soup, a bottle of alcohol, assorted biscuits, rich coffee, and creamy chocolate.

"Thank you. Would you like to come in?"

I had to restrain myself from smiling. This was exactly what I had hoped for.

I followed him inside and settled onto the sofa. The house was even more grimy and neglected than before, layers of dust and clutter casting a sombre shadow over the room.

"I'm sorry, I didn't have a chance to clean. There was a mix-up, and my electricity was cut off, so I couldn't vacuum," Miroslav said, his voice tinged with embarrassment as he gestured apologetically at the cluttered room. Dust motes floated lazily in the shafts of light that pierced the dim space.

"It's fine," I replied, a smile playing at the corners of my lips, though I kept it hidden.

"Would you like a coffee?" he offered, his voice hopeful. The coffee table between us was crowded with empty beer bottles, their labels peeling slightly.

I hesitated, momentarily considering joining him, but opted for something else. "Just water," I finally said.

He returned, the floorboards creaking under his weight, with a cold beer for himself and a glass of water for me.

"I'm so sorry about Lux. He was such a good dog," I said, nodding towards the photograph on the mantelpiece, the frame slightly askew. The image captured Lux mid-run, ears flapping in the wind, eyes bright with joy.

"He was my only friend. To Lux, the best dog a man could have," Miroslav said, lifting his bottle in a solemn toast. His voice cracked slightly as he spoke, and he took a long drink, the liquid disappearing swiftly down his throat.

"Did you recover the body?"

He nodded, a shadow passing over his features. "I buried him in the backyard, under the fig tree. He loved eating those figs. Then he would shit like a hose, and I'd find patches of diarrhoea all around the backyard," he said with a wry chuckle, breaking the sombre mood.

I barked with laughter, the unexpected humour lightening the atmosphere.

He smiled, the corners of his eyes crinkling, though a trace of sadness lingered.

"Pets give us so much love and so much trouble," I remarked, sipping the cool water that refreshed my dry throat.

He nodded, his gaze distant.

"I'm glad you found his body. It would be hard to grieve without knowing where he was or having somewhere to mourn him," I continued, my voice soft with empathy.

He nodded again, sinking deeper into his armchair, as if trying to merge with its worn fabric, the weight of the world pressing heavily upon him.

"I wanted to ask you something, but... Never mind. Now is not the time," I said, hesitating as I felt the conversation shift.

He looked up, curiosity piqued. "Ask. If I can, I'll answer," he replied, his voice inviting.

"What happened in Srebrenica? I heard from some women speaking to my father that you were there. That you spoke about what happened at a wedding," I ventured, the words leaving my mouth cautiously.

"Fucking Branko," Miroslav muttered under his breath, his expression darkening as he drained the rest of his beer. "That idiot doesn't know what he's talking about, and then he incited me," he added, his voice tinged with frustration.

I waited, my body tense, my eyes flicking to the backpack where the gun's reassuring weight lay hidden. The act of reciprocity—the gift basket I had offered him earlier—seemed to hang in the air between us, an unspoken bond urging him to reveal more.

"I made the mistake of speaking about what happened in the mother country, and it's haunted me ever since," he admitted, his voice heavy with regret as he took another sip of his beer, the glass clinking softly against his teeth.

I exhaled a deep, trembling sigh of relief and waited, my heart pounding, hoping that he would continue.

His eyes, shadowed by memories too heavy to bear, began his confession. "We were forced out after our village was cleansed," he continued. "Given a house that belonged to someone else who'd been driven out. Everything stolen. Destroyed. I wondered if my own home had been taken the same way." He stopped. "We were all just chess pieces," he said. "Moved around by politicians who never paid the price."

I knew that truth already. Ramo and I had said it many times. The powerful survived. Everyone else carried the damage.

I reminded myself he had not yet arrived at Potočari, and it was all too easy for him to cast himself as a victim.

"I joined the army and was made a driver after a basic course. Before the war, I drove buses," he said. "When fighting started, they needed drivers for trucks and equipment. I joined for revenge. That didn't last. What I saw isn't something a young girl should hear." He paused, lifting a cigarette in his rough fingers.

I knew too well what he spoke of—the concentration camp at Omarska, where Muslim men were subjected to unspeakable psychological and physical torture, forced to commit acts so inhumane against their kin for the cruel amusement of Serb soldiers. And the rape camps... Those terrible places where women were trapped and repeatedly violated, a vicious attempt to taint the purity of the Muslim bloodline. I had heard these stories whispered in hushed tones during the war and had read the harrowing details in the newspapers as the Tribunal dragged on.

"Then came Potočari," he murmured.

My grip tightened on my backpack, finding comfort in the gun concealed within. A dangerous thought crept into my mind: would he remember the young girl he had tormented? I almost dared to hope he would so that I could justify shooting him as self-defence. I knew, rationally, that my thoughts were a tangled web of contradictions—how could I justify the presence bringing the gun and then claim self-defence—yet the daydreams continued.

"We were told that the Muslims were being cleansed—that the buses were there to transport them out of the complex," Miroslav continued, his voice growing heavy with resignation as he gripped his beer bottle with white-knuckled intensity and stared blankly at the scarred surface of the coffee table. "In truth, those commanding us knew the bitter reality, but for us foot soldiers, we were only given the half-truths we needed to swallow."

I clenched my teeth, forcing myself to stay quiet.

"When we arrived, the Muslims were packed into the cold factory buildings, silent, terrified, waiting for whatever would come next. I barely remember that first night. We drank until we felt nothing. I went with the men on a hunting trip, hoping to steal jewellery to give my family a chance at a new life. But they took a young girl—no older than my daughter. And what they did to her—"

He stopped, his face folding in on itself, his head dropping toward the table. He didn't need to say more. I remembered her clearly: the blood on her thighs, her body hanging from the beams. She still haunted me. What was done to her could just as easily have been done to me.

I strained to piece together the fragments of that dreadful night. According to his recollection, he had been with the pack that descended upon us like wolves. They hunted me too; I recalled their hungry eyes fixating on my necklace, and the moment they discovered it was silver, they lost interest. Then, as they decided to take me, he had been among them. Soon after, another girl was taken, which was when he claimed to have left. I hadn't seen any of it myself.

"I couldn't bear to watch any longer," he continued, his voice heavy with regret. "I returned to the bus I was meant to drive, and stayed there for the rest of the night."

The next day, I too remembered the cacophony—the relentless hum of the bus engine, the oppressive heat seeping into every corner as we shuffled forward on our uncertain journey. Women and girls sat trembling among us, their tears and soft, frightened sniffles etched into the stifling air. There was a constant, unspoken fear: were we truly being transported to a sanctuary of freedom, or would our bus be ominously diverted off course? I recalled glimpsing other vehicles departing from the main road, disappearing into narrow side streets, while elsewhere, buses halted abruptly to unload women onto empty stretches of roadside. How many innocent women had truly reached safety?

"I was told they had to interrogate the men, to use them as bargaining chips," he said flatly. "I wasn't stupid. I knew they would be killed—after all, they had Serb blood on their hands. Still, I believed we Serbs had some mercy left."

He stopped, glanced at me, then kept going. I couldn't tell if he was telling the truth or reshaping it to ease his guilt, but I was glad he didn't stop.

"It wasn't until I drove the first bus to an empty field and saw the bulldozers digging a mass grave that I understood," he said. "After the men got off, I was ordered back to Potočari for another load. Gunfire echoed while I drove. I kept my eyes on the road."

He spoke like someone trying to excuse himself—as if driving meant he wasn't responsible. But he was. I tightened my grip on my gun.

"I don't know how many trips I made," he said quietly. "I still dream of that road. The heat. The bus full of fear."

I knew then I would make him pay. I saw Ramo in my mind—young, untouched, looking out at the land that would bury him.

"When my last bus emptied, I thought it was over," he said. "I wanted to go home. Then my commander stopped me. He told me to step outside and said, 'Now you shoot one.' I'd killed before, but never like that. I fired without looking. I told myself it wasn't really me."

His voice shook. "Then he took me to the pit. A young man sat there—about your age. I said I couldn't do it. He was the age of my daughters. So my commander shot him. Then he pointed to an old man. 'Shoot him,' he said. 'He won't live much longer.' I froze. He threatened my wife and daughters. I had no choice. I closed my eyes and fired. I heard the shot. Then the thud."

A shiver ran down my spine, every nerve on high alert, while Miroslav's gaze darted to my left, as if haunted by a memory only he could see.

"I'm so sorry. I'm so sorry I killed you," he whispered, his voice cracking with remorse.

In that moment, I understood the phantom he spoke of—a ghost from the past that clung to him just as it did to me. None of us had emerged from the war without scars.

"After that, it felt unreal," he said. "I was made to wait while bulldozers buried the bodies in the pit. Then I drove the other soldiers home. One of them complained that his finger hurt from shooting too many *Balije*."

I wiped my face absentmindedly, realising with a quiet shock that my cheeks were wet with tears—tears I hadn't even noticed falling.

"When I came home, I tried to forget. But soon there were rumours about Srebrenica—claims that the Muslims had made it all up, that nothing had really happened. I stayed silent until one night in a bar, when I heard three men laughing about it. I couldn't take it anymore. I told them, *I was there. I saw it happen.* They laughed and chased me out. That night, my commander came to my house with men from the unit. They beat me until I was covered in blood. Before they left, they warned me: if I ever spoke again, they wouldn't beat me—they would kill me."

Was that threat the truth, or just a story to ease his guilt? I thought of his wife's letter—the reason they fled, the reason he was branded a traitor. Maybe the truth was there, between the lines.

"My wife looked after me. Those months were hard." He drank from his beer. "They broke my arm and ribs and damaged my leg. I couldn't work, and we struggled to feed our daughters. My wife was angry. She didn't care if there had been a massacre. She said the Muslims chased us out and got what they deserved. She told me if I ever spoke about it again, she would leave. So I stopped. We came to Australia on a refugee visa. I wanted to get away from the people who treated me like a liar."

I realised how much alike we were. We all came here looking for a fresh start, yet our pasts would never leave us. We were all carrying our ghosts and pain.

"When we got to Australia, my wife made me go to church. I hated it. The priest got up and denied the genocide—he'd never even been to our country, never seen the war. I told her I wouldn't go back to listen to that rubbish. After that, rumours spread. One night, a brick came through our window. Written on it were the words: Miroslav = Coward. That was the last straw for her."

He glanced at the photo of his wife and daughters. "She told me she could no longer bear our life together. Grabbing the girls, she left for Queensland to live with her sister."

I remembered discovering the brick boxed away.

"Some days I blame her for leaving, for looking away. Other days I understand her need to escape. I feel it too. But every night the old man comes to me, standing by my bed, watching as I sleep. I can't let the memories—or the ghosts—go."

A chill ran through me as he spoke, his voice shaking. He kept scanning the room, as if something was watching him. Had the war finally broken him? Then again, I spoke to Ramo in the dark too.

"Why not tell the authorities?" I asked, keeping my voice steady.

"I thought about it," he said. "I almost did. But my wife stopped me. She said it would put our daughters in danger. I have to protect them."

"And what about doing the right thing?" I said. "What about the families still waiting, hoping for answers?" I thought of my father, of Ramo, of all the others. There was no closure—only pain.

"No one is innocent in war," Miroslav said, finishing his beer. "Everyone gets blood on their hands."

"Most of those 8,000 weren't soldiers," I said. "They were ordinary men and boys."

"I've told you enough," he said. "Your friend's father is buried somewhere out there. He's dead. They're all dead. Everyone has to find a way to live with it."

It was easy for him to talk about peace. For him, it was just a way to walk away from the pain. "I don't know how you live with yourself," I whispered.

"Neither do I," he said quietly, meeting my eyes. For a moment, the pain there shook me.

I briefly thought of pulling my gun and ending it. Instead, I stopped myself. I had what I came for.

He stood, and I followed. I wanted to argue, but his face told me it was pointless. He had justified everything to himself. Survival. Self-preservation.

What he needed was a reason to speak.

He walked me to the door. I left.

At the tram stop, I took out the tape recorder and rewound it with shaking hands. His voice played back, flat and cold: No one is innocent in war. *Everyone gets blood on their hands.*

Relief and grief hit me at once. I had him.

On the tram, I listened again and again. Then I rewound the tape and recorded over the beginning—his greeting, the moment he said Zora's name.

Now the tape held only what mattered. His words. His truth.

16-Exposure

I paced in the lobby of Alyssa's office building, keeping an eye on the elevators. The elevator dinged open, and Alyssa stepped out. Her eyes glanced off me until I called her name.

"Seka, they told me you were waiting," Alyssa said when she came out. She looked at my blonde hair with surprise.

"I have something for you." I held out the tape recorder. "Can we speak privately?"

Alyssa nodded and led me into the lift. When we reached the floor where the newspaper was located, we walked past frantic men and women on computers, chatter in the air, palpable tension as they wrote to meet the daily deadline of a national newspaper.

As I followed, I caught sight of myself in the glass of a conference room, the light making it look like a mirror. My eyes were blue. I forgot to take out my contact lenses. No wonder Alyssa didn't recognise me.

Alyssa walked into a small meeting room. "Did you want something to drink?" She gestured to a chair.

I shook my head. I wanted this over and done with quickly. We sat, and I turned on the tape recorder. The interview with Miroslav began playing. Alyssa's eyes widened, and she jotted notes on her notepad with a pen, a funny handwriting that looked like some symbols. I'd asked her about it in Srebrenica, and she told me it was called shorthand, a form of dictation to write down notes that could be transcribed quickly.

"How did you come by this?" she asked sharply as the interview recording clicked off, her tone edged with suspicion.

"He lost his dog and wandered into my veterinary surgery," I explained, my voice low and measured. "We started talking as fellow former Yugoslavs. In his loneliness, he needed a friend."

Alyssa's eyes swept over me, scrutinising every detail from my meticulously styled hair to my worn boots. "And he's aware of your true identity? That you lost family in Srebrenica?" she pressed.

I offered a slow, deliberate nod, my face betraying nothing.

Her next question cut through the tension: "Is there a reason you've changed your hair and eye colour?"

"I just wanted a change," I replied, self-consciously smoothing my bob away from my face.

"Is that the whole story?" she asked, leaning in.

"Of course," I said, tapping the tape recorder as if punctuating my words. "So, when do you plan to publish the article?"

"It's not that simple," Alyssa countered, carefully placing her pen beside the neatly arranged notepad. "Did Miroslav consent to being recorded?"

I blinked in confusion. "What do you mean?"

"Did you ask him for permission to record this interview?"

I shook my head slowly.

"It's illegal to record someone without their consent," she reminded me.

I could feel the heat and constriction in my chest, a slow-burning anger that flushed my skin as I clenched my fists under the table. "You mean to say that it's illegal to record someone even if they confess to murder?" I shot back, gripping the edge of the conference table.

"Yes," she said.

"What if he agrees to go on the record?" I asked.

"If I call him right now, will he consent?" she nodded toward the phone in the conference room.

Scenarios whirled in my head. If Alyssa contacted Miroslav, mentioning she was following up on the information I, Seka Torlak, had provided her, he'd soon discover I'd been working undercover. Miroslav was a man tormented by inner conflict—a struggle between conscience and loyalty. Would he even agree to be interviewed by a national newspaper?

I shook my head slowly at the thought.

"How did you get this information?" she continued, not letting up.

"I told him that I was Zora Đokić," I admitted softly.

"Alright," she responded, leaning back slightly. "So he doesn't know your real identity?"

I shook my head once more.

"What you did was incredibly dangerous," Alyssa warned. "Who knows how he might have reacted had he discovered the truth?"

I glanced at my backpack, a small comfort coming from the gun inside. I had no fear of Miroslav.

"I don't need you to protect me," I stated firmly. "I need you to do your job. So tell me—when are you going to publish the article?"

"I'm still in the process of corroborating the evidence," Alyssa replied.

"There's no need to delay," I insisted sharply. "You heard him—he can't return to Serbia and simply hide out. We must publish now, so more people feel compelled to come forward."

"It's not that simple—" she began once more.

"It's not that hard," I interjected.

"I know you're frustrated, but we need to do this properly," she said. "If you have more details that could help me, now is the time to share them."

I paused, feeling the rush of conflicting emotions. I had painstakingly gathered every scrap of information about his military service, marriage, and personal documents. Each piece was meticulously noted, ready to be handed over to Alyssa. Yet now, a sudden shadow of doubt crept in—should I give it to her? Revealing that I had broken into his house to collect it would doom the information to be rejected.

Taking a shaky breath, I continued, "He told me the name of his commander and detailed his army service when we talked before I started recording our conversation." I recounted every word, watching as she diligently scribbled notes down.

"I'm going to continue working on this," she declared. "I'll publish an article that exposes him."

"When?'" My voice came out sharp, laced with impatience. "It's been a month and nothing has happened."

"These things take time. I promise you, I'm doing the work." She gathered her notepad and pen, preparing to leave the table. Then, with sincere concern, she added, "In the meantime, you must promise me you'll stay away from him. He could be dangerous."

I couldn't help but feel a mix of defiance and resignation. "You do your job, and I'll do mine."

"Seka, this isn't your job—it's mine," she insisted softly, taking my hand in hers. "You've already been through too much. Leave this to the professionals for now."

I forced a bitter smile. "So, I can just wait another four years?"

Her mouth opened to protest, but I had already turned away. "Thanks for nothing," I muttered, grabbing my worn backpack as I stalked out of the office.

If Alyssa wasn't going to act quickly, then I would. I felt the surge of urgency pulsing through me—I had to seize this momentum to expose him. I boarded the train home, lost in my thoughts.

How would I manoeuvre to bring him down? I knew I had to be cautious. The memory of that shattered brick through the window haunted me. I planned to turn his own people against him. It wouldn't be too difficult—they were a rabble, volatile and ready to turn on anyone who crossed their path.

A sinister plan began to crystallise in my mind.

Unbeknownst to Miroslav, he had unwittingly handed me the key to his destruction.

Upon arriving home, I spent the remainder of the night hunched over my computer, drafting and redrafting an article in my mother tongue.

A true witness—The Serb with a conscience by Seka Torlak

The Serbs claim that we, the Bosniaks of Srebrenica are lying about what happened on the 11 July 1995. That there was no way that over 8,000 of our men and boys could have been killed and buried in mass graves. As proof, they offer the fact that it would have taken numerous buses and many trips to achieve this aim. And they are right.

An operation such as this took many months of planning to work. It took many buses, it took bus drivers, it took earth-moving equipment. And it was a concentrated effort to ensure that the Bosniaks from Srebrenica would never return, thus yielding this mineral rich and highly coveted piece of land to the Serbs.

But they don't need to believe our people. They can ask one of their own. Miroslav Vlahović was there on that day. Originally from Medeno Polje, Miroslav and his wife Gordana were cleansed from their village by the Bosniak fighters during a military action to join Srebrenica to the free territory of Tuzla and create a safe corridor for transport of food.

Miroslav, with his family, two daughters Ljubica and Marica, then went to live in their mother country of Serbia. He joined the Serbian army, where his skills as a bus driver were put to use to transport weapons and soldiers.

On the 11 July 1995, he was at Potočari among the frightened refugees who gathered there seeking shelter. He needed to set up a new life for himself and his family by emigrating from Serbia. The necklace glinting at my throat caught his eye, for he was hunting for gold and jewellery, what he saw as his recompense for losing his home to Bosniaks.

I was a frightened Bosniak girl wearing a silver coin that was minted to commemorate Tito's birthday. When Miroslav saw that my trinket was no more than a relic of our dead Yugoslavia, he threw it upon the floor and gifted it to me as a memento to remember my beloved Silver City.

Miroslav was there as a bus driver, and he ferried busloads of men and boys from Potočari to the killing fields. And when he delivered his last bus load, his commander ordered him to kill one of the men and to implicate himself.

When he returned home, he was pricked by his conscience and suffered a beating in retribution. He fled to Australia to get away from his compatriots in arms who viewed his conscience as a liability, and when confronted with genocide deniers in his new community, he spoke up. His home was targeted and vandalised. His wife and children left to live in Queensland and away from further reprisals.

When I caught the number 82 bus and recognised Miroslav as one of the perpetrators at Potočari Industrial Complex and confronted him, Miroslav admitted that he was troubled by the acts of the war and that he struggled to live with his conscience. He is a man caught between his conscience and his fear, but he still found the courage to speak up and tell the truth, to admit his part in the wrongdoing.

Now that he has come forward with the truth and shared what he knows about the mass graves, some of our people will have their bodies recovered. Miroslav is a true Yugoslav, one who does not believe in the murder of innocent citizens. If only we had more people like him, this conflict might not have happened.

Miroslav had nowhere to run. He couldn't return to Serbia, where he was already a pariah for speaking the truth. He might try to escape to Queensland to escape the wrath of his community, but even then, he would still be available to the authorities for arrest.

I looked at the letter I had swiped from his daughters to him. And even if he did go to Queensland, I would still be on his trail. Ready for retribution.

If his community threw a brick at his house for speaking out, how would they react to the thought that he had spoken to a Bosniak outside of the community and told them the truth?

All I had to do was sit back and watch the sparks fly, and his whole world come crashing down. The only concern was breaking my cover, but I could even avoid that by removing the coin.

I felt tingles as I sealed the envelope, with Miroslav's phone number in the letter, telling the journalist to call him and confirm the details.

The woman who owned the Bosnian newspaper would love an article like this. I doubted she would even contact Miroslav to confirm the story, but he would be caught off guard if she did. She had too many details to confirm. She would be so eager to publish an anti-Serb story. And once it was published, it would be out.

There was one thing left to do before the newspaper came out. I burned all the notes I had about Miroslav's personal life. There couldn't be any evidence in the house.

I carried the burek to the dining table slowly, careful not to let it tumble as Mama and Emir finished their prayers in the quiet of their bedrooms. My hands shook as I placed the pastry before them.

"What's with you?" Emir snapped, catching the burek just as it threatened to slide off his plate.

"I need to talk to you both about something," I said, wiping the lingering dough from my hands before sitting down.

Emir began tearing into the warm, soft pita with his calloused fingers, while Mama gracefully cut herself a small, neat piece with her well-used knife and fork. The clink of cutlery and the soft rustle of paper filled the otherwise hushed room. "Do you remember the bad man in Potočari who tried to steal my necklace?" I asked.

Mama's face darkened as she nodded briefly, her eyes distant with recollections. Emir's gaze narrowed sharply. I could sense the painful flashbacks of his ordeal at Potočari—a time when he was forced to navigate the treacherous Bosnian countryside during the relentless Death March, evading Serbian pursuers with nothing but sheer will. After reuniting in Tuzla, we had shared just the surface of our suffering, never fully unravelling the true horror lurking behind our scars.

In a hushed whisper that barely cut the heavy air, I admitted, "I saw the man in Australia." Immediately, Emir stopped chewing; his fork hovered mid-air as an eerie silence enveloped us.

"I've been working with Alyssa Jones to expose him and report his actions to The Hague," I continued. "But the process was too slow, so I wrote a newspaper article that will be published in the Bosnian community paper." I pushed a crisp, hard copy of my article toward them.

"He confessed?" Emir asked. I nodded stiffly.

"Why isn't Alyssa publishing about him?" Mama asked.

"She is. We just thought that getting the story out in the Bosnian paper first would encourage others to come forward, and that would pressure authorities into issuing an arrest warrant."

"What day was he on this bus?" Emir asked.

I could almost read his thoughts—he was determined to track down Miroslav and exact his form of justice. "I can't remember," I lied.

"I'll find out," he declared, setting the paper down roughly on the table before storming out of the house.

"Where are you going?" Mama called after him.

"To see friends," he replied curtly, climbing into his car. The vehicle roared to life and screeched away.

Mama turned to me, frustration evident in her furrowed brow. "You shouldn't have published the article," she scolded, crumpling the paper with a swift, irate motion and tossing it out the door. "Now your brother is bound to do something stupid."

I tried to protest, "Miroslav isn't working tonight."

"You'd better be right, otherwise your brother might end up in jail." With a final huff, Mama retreated to her bedroom, closing the door behind her.

I quickly slipped on my shoes and bolted out the door, my footsteps echoing along the dim, quiet street. My trembling hands fumbled with the coin-operated payphone, and after three painstaking tries, I dialled Miroslav's number. When he answered, a wave of relief washed over me.

"The Bosnians know who you are and where you work," I warned gruffly. "You can't go back to work or they'll kill you." I ended the call abruptly, heart pounding fiercely. Almost immediately, the phone rang again—a callback triggered by Miroslav's code. I sat in the cramped booth until the line finally went silent. This careful measure was exactly why I never called from home, ensuring no one else would overhear. I returned home and spent the night on the couch, watching crappy TV as I waited for Emir to come home. He arrived at midnight, his eyes red-rimmed, his body defeated.

Mama heard the front door and ran to him, hugging him. "My son, you scared me so much." She held him tightly, as if she would never let him go.

Emir met my gaze over her shoulder. His stare was burning with hatred. My skin broke out into goose pimples. I had to ensure Emir never found Miroslav, or I would lose another family member.

When the article was finally published the following week, my mother was inundated with phone calls from Bosnians scattered across Victoria. The tension was palpable, with whispers of retribution buzzing through the air like an electric current, as people attempted to trace him through intricate networks. It seemed inevitable that a Bosnian or a Serb would eventually find him and deliver their form of justice.

I carefully scanned the newspaper article, translating it into English, before sending it to Alyssa via email. I added a note that read, "Now that Miroslav needs friends, he might be ready to talk." Her response was swift, suggesting we needed to have a conversation, and we set a time to meet.

When we spoke, her voice carried a tone of irritation and stress. "You took matters into your own hands, and now I'm scrambling," she said, her frustration clear.

"Did you speak to him?" I inquired. "Is he willing to go on the record?"

"He's thinking about it," she admitted, though her tone was begrudging.

"So it worked. This might be the break we need," I noted, hopeful.

"What you did was dangerous, and now he knows who you are, too. Have you thought about that? He's a man with nothing to lose who has already admitted to being a killer. What if he comes after you?" she questioned.

I reached into my drawer, my fingers brushing against the cold metal of the gun, and I caressed it thoughtfully. "I hope he does," I replied, a hint of defiance in my voice.

"Do you have a death wish?" Alyssa shouted.

"Maybe I do," I murmured, glancing into the mirror and catching sight of my blonde hair. It was time for Seka to make her return. Zora had completed her mission. "Keep me updated," I said before breaking off the call.

17-Roar

I called Phuong-Vy to arrange a time for her to restore my hair colour. Her phone picked up, but there was only a heavy, expectant silence on the other end. "Hello, Phuong-Vy, is that you?" I asked.

"Seka?" Her voice trembled with apprehension.

"What's the matter?" I asked, my hand tightening around the handset.

"I think someone is outside watching me," she whispered, each word laced with fear.

I pictured her in her cosy bungalow, anxiously peering through the blinds into the backyard, her eyes wide with terror as she clutched the phone.

"I'm coming over. Don't go outside," I reassured her.

I hurried to the backyard, gathering Lux, and led him to Ninu's truck, which I had parked discreetly around the block to keep Mama unaware.

Walking down her driveway, I saw a cigarette tip glowing ominously from a tree in front of the bungalow. Lux tensed, growled deep in his throat, and lunged towards the shadowy figure. I unclipped his lead, releasing him into action. In that moment, a piercing scream shattered the stillness, and

I recognised Tom's voice muttering curses. Screeching tyres echoed in the air before Lux trotted back to my side, his head held high.

"Good boy," I murmured as I walked towards the bungalow. The lights inside flicked on, and I called out Phuong-Vy's name.

She opened the door slowly, gripping a cold, metal pole tightly in her hands. "What was that noise?" she asked, her eyes darting around the darkened yard.

"That was Tom meeting Lux," I explained, patting the dog affectionately beside me.

"He was out here," she said softly as she stepped forward, raising the metal pole like a makeshift weapon to ward off any lingering threat.

"Not anymore," I replied.

Her gaze fell to Lux, and her expression softened instantly. Gently, she set the pole aside near the door and wrapped her arms around the dog's neck. "My hero," she whispered.

Inviting me inside, she led the way and Lux promptly claimed a spot on the rug in front of the glowing TV, his ears twitching as if absorbing every sound of our conversation.

I noticed the exhaustion lining Phuong-Vy's face. "Have you slept at all?" I asked, concern threading through my voice.

She shook her head slowly. "Every night, I hear footsteps outside my house. I see nothing but darkness when I muster the courage to pull aside the curtains. And then my phone rings—empty voices, silence when I answer—so I hang up. I keep receiving pizza deliveries from various shops. They show up with ten pizzas at a time, and when I tell them I didn't order anything, the delivery drivers hurl insults at me. Soon after, the shops called to tell me I was banned from ordering." She sounded so defeated and broken as she spoke.

"I've been plagued by bills arriving in the mail, accusing me of subscribing to services I never asked for. One day, it's a book club, the next, it's a magazine, then Tupperware, and then candles. Just as I cancel one subscription, another seems to take its place. And today, a credit statement arrived, declaring that a credit card was opened in my name and has been accumulating charges daily. When I went to the bank to clarify that I never applied for such a card, they insisted that I did. Now I'm forced to pay a minimum repayment, or the debt collectors will come after me. I can't even figure out how to begin fixing this mess."

Wrapping my arm around her shoulders, I held her close, letting her know she wasn't alone. I handed her a tissue, and she wiped her face.

"Why didn't you call me?" I asked.

"At first, it was so small. It seemed more of an annoyance, and I thought he'd get it out of his system. Then things just kept escalating, and today I received the credit card statement, and it's just so much."

That prick Tom was diabolical. He was too scared to stalk her, so now he'd upped the ante and was terrorising her in other ways. Ways that kept him safe from harm and fucked up her life.

We spent the day going to the police, getting a fraudulent account set up, and getting the government to realise it was a case of mistaken identity. My rage burned brighter and brighter. That prick Tom needed to be brought down a peg or two.

I wasn't going to let him get away with destroying Phuong-Vy. The squirrelly bastard had never shown Phuong-Vy where he lived. He was like a ghost. But I knew his weakness. His regular hunting ground.

I slept over at Phuong-Vy's and distracted her with a girls' night. She dyed my hair back to brown, and we watched movies. I told her I had to stay home the next night and left Lux with her.

The next night, I drove to the city in Ninu's truck. I went to Metro and scouted the lay of the land. Sure enough, I found him on his usual floor, doing his business. I knew from our nights out that he would be out until the early hours of the morning. I waited and watched for him to have a glass. He ordered a drink and left it on the bar table while chatting with a brunette. As I walked past, I saw she was Asian. The bastard had a type. He fetishised Asian chicks. I quickly tilted my hand over his drink, pouring in the vial. I'd borrowed some ketamine from the vet clinic. I went to stand in the corner and waited. Tom slugged the drink. I could see the exact moment it took effect. He began moving slowly, his face looking blank and slightly dopey. The girl spoke to him a few times and walked off in a huff.

I put down my drink and walked over to him. "Howdy, ho, Tom," I said, putting his arm around my shoulders. "Why don't we get out of here."

He didn't respond. Ketamine was used on humans as a sedative, while on animals it was a tranquilliser. He wouldn't remember what happened as it brought about amnesia and a dissociated state. I'd first learned about ketamine when I was in Srebrenica, and doctors desperate for pain relief and anaesthetic dipped into any medication they had. When I began working at the vet clinic and saw it was an animal anaesthetic, I found it interesting how desperate we'd been.

Now it would do me good. Tom would be pliable and go wherever I wanted, and I would be able to teach him a lesson.

I walked him to the parking garage where I had Ninu's truck and sat him in the passenger seat. I drove to the western suburbs and the quarry that had just closed down off Duke Street. Tom slept as I drove, his head bouncing against the passenger window. He fell into me a few times when I took the curves, and I had to push him back upright. When we reached our destination, he was still out.

I yanked him roughly from the truck and hauled him forward into the glare of the headlights, each step unsteady as he struggled under my grip. I had parked on the crumbling edge of the quarry, where the inky darkness of the massive earthen hole stretched out before us like a hungry void. The quarry was desolate, a barren wasteland torn apart by ruthless earthmovers that had ravaged the land. What remained was nothing short of a gaping wound in the earth, as if Mother Nature were plotting retribution. In her wrath, Tom was would be a worthy sacrifice.

As he began to stir, his eyelids flickering open, I rifled through his pockets and pulled out a neat stack of bills. I counted them methodically in the dim light, confirming it would be enough for Phuong-Vy to settle the credit card debt he'd accumulated in her name.

Slowly coming to consciousness, he sat up gingerly, cradling his aching head as confusion writhed across his features. "Where am I?" he murmured, his voice rough with disorientation. Pushing himself to stand, he teetered alarmingly close to the quarry's scarred edge, sending small pebbles cascading down the rocky side.

The brilliant headlights scalded his face, causing him to flinch as he twisted away from the burning light. "Who are you?" he demanded, his voice trembling slightly.

I stepped forward from behind the truck. "Seka, what the fuck are you doing?" Tom shouted.

"You crossed the line by messing with my friend," I replied coldly. "Now it's time I mess with you."

"What the fuck is wrong with you? You can't do anything to me," he sneered, taking an aggressive step towards me.

Calmly, I reached for the gun resting at my side and levelled it at him. "Are you sure about that?" I taunted.

Tom's face drained of colour. "I thought you'd thrown it away," he stammered.

"I lied," I admitted with a dark chuckle. "I needed a gun; I wanted something to scare off guys like you."

"You're not really going to shoot, are you? You don't even know how," he quipped with a smirk.

I returned his smirk with one of my own, as I gestured with the weapon toward a weathered sign half-obscured by dust and decay. The sign, boldly declaring the territory as Caine Property, featured an oversized letter "A" marred by a crude bullet hole. "See that sign?" I asked, nodding slowly. "Do you think I could hit the 'A'?"

"Sure. Go ahead and give it a shot," he challenged.

Taking a deliberate stance with my feet planted wide for support, I aimed carefully and pulled the trigger. The explosion of the gunshot echoed violently throughout the quarry, a thunderous assault on our ears that reverberated off the walls of the chasm. Tom jerked back, instinctively ducking.

"I guess you really don't know anything about women," I sneered.

He glanced at the sign, his eyes widening in astonishment as he took in the stark bullet hole piercing the triangle of the "A."

"I'm a top shot. And if you try anything—anything at all," I warned with a dramatic sweep of the gun, "you'll find out very quickly that messing with my friend has consequences."

"What? I haven't done a damn thing," he protested, his voice faltering.

I lifted the gun again, now targeting his leg. "So, do you want me to put a hole in you, or are you ready to start telling the truth?"

"God, please, don't..." he whimpered, shrinking back. "Okay, okay, I've been crank-calling her," he finally confessed in a choked rush of words.

"And?" I prompted.

He hesitated and repeated his confession with a trembling "And?" full of dread at what might come next.

Without further delay, I fired again—this time, the bullet skittered near his feet. Startled, he leapt up and screamed, his cry piercing the still night. "Scream all you want," I warned ominously. "No one will hear you out here. I could fill you up with bullet holes and roll your corpse off this edge, and no one would be the wiser."

His eyes darted around in frantic terror as realisation sank in: I had fired two bullets, and no help was coming. "Okay, yes, I've been fucking with her—I signed her up for services."

"She was right to dump you. You're scum," I spat back. I squeezed the trigger once more, sending a searing bullet straight near his other foot. The metallic report of the shot shattered the silence. He leapt back, a scream bursting from him.

As his body trembled and tears began to stream down his face, a heady surge of power coursed through me. He was at my mercy.

"Yes, she was right to dump me. I'm scum," he cried out in a ragged, pleading voice, "I'm sorry, I promise I won't do it again."

I lifted my arm slowly, the cold metal of my gun glinting under the low light as I aimed steadily at his chest. "You see, I want to believe you," I said, "but I don't know if I can. You're a vicious little fucker. For her sake, and mine, I think I should just kill you now."

Desperation bled into his voice as he pleaded, "No, please don't! I'll go away. I'll leave Melbourne. She'll never hear from me again."

"I don't know if I can trust you." I reached over and retrieved a heavy, worn bag from the passenger seat. As I opened it, its contents spilled out: his driver's licence, his house keys, and other personal tokens of the life he once lived. "I went through your wallet and found your driver's licence and keys. I even visited that dump you call home and packed up all your shit. Your roommate was asleep so I left him a note in your handwriting—it was so convenient that I also stumbled upon your address book in your bedside table. Your note warned that some dangerous people were after you and that you had to lie low. Everything is right here. All I have to do is chuck this bag—and your body—off the edge, and soon enough, no one will miss you. By the time they realise you're gone, so much time will have passed that no one will remember the fucker you were."

I nodded grimly toward the hefty weights resting beside me. "And when I weigh your corpse down with these, your body won't see the light of day for months. You'll be nothing more than a forgotten name by the time it's discovered. And this gun, well—this gun can never be traced back to me. It's a perfect crime, and you, my friend, are a perfect asshole."

"Please, I won't do it again. I'll vanish—I have family in Sydney. I'll catch a bus tonight, and I'll disappear. I swear I'll never come back to Melbourne."

I sneered at his desperate assurances. "How do I know you'll keep your word? How do I know you'll leave and never darken these streets again?"

"I promise. I just want to live free. I don't want to die." He was on his knees, hands clasped, begging.

I held the gun, pointed, without saying anything. There was a part of me that wanted to pull the trigger. To see what it was like to kill. Tom was scum, killing him was cleaning the earth of the plague. So many good people died, why should he get to live? It was like I was being taken over by evil. Not pulling the trigger was so hard. I had to fight with all my strength not to pull.

"Please," he implored, his voice trembling with desperation. Then his posture crumbled, his shoulders sagging as defeat washed over him. Urine stained the front of his jeans. If I pulled the trigger now, I would be no different from the men who had mercilessly taken my family from me.

"You do know that if you go after my friend again, if she encounters any more trouble, or even senses the slightest threat, I will come for you. And this time, there will be no second chances," I warned, my voice low and steady.

"Okay. Okay," he replied, his voice barely a whisper as he nodded in agreement.

I nudged the bag toward him with my foot. "Change your pants and toss that pair over the edge."

He turned his back to me, hurriedly changing into clean clothes, his movements awkward and hurried. "What are you going to do to me?" he asked, a quiver of fear in his voice.

"I'm driving you to the bus station. You're going to leave and never come back," I stated firmly.

He nodded, sniffling as he wiped his nose with the back of his hand.

"You drive." I directed him to sit in the driver's seat while I positioned myself in the passenger seat, the gun resting loosely in my grip.

We drove silently to Southern Cross, the tension palpable between us. Once there, I shadowed him into the station, handing him a few bills from the bundle I had confiscated from him, ensuring he had enough to buy a ticket. Together, we approached the bus platform.

"I'm keeping the rest to settle what you owe her," I informed him. He nodded, mute and acquiescent.

I watched as he boarded the bus, his footsteps heavy. He didn't glance back, even as he walked down the aisle, disappearing into the vehicle.

I drove home, expecting to feel relief for resolving Phuong-Vy's predicament. Instead, a fiery rage simmered within me, an insatiable hunger for revenge that gnawed at my insides. It was as if a dormant thirst for vengeance had been awakened, urging me toward a darker path. I had crossed to the dark side and was flirting with evil, but I didn't care.

18-Birthday

I was wearing a new dress, soft pink and flowing gracefully around my hips. It felt like a fresh start, a symbol of shedding the remnants of Zora's ghost, and it was the first time Ninu would see me with my brown hair again. I felt more like myself than ever before.

Emir pulled up in his car, dropping me off at the house. I carefully retrieved Lux from the backseat, the leash cool in my hand. I had told Emir I was heading to a friend's birthday party and that Lux would be a birthday gift. He accepted my explanation without question.

Glancing at the house, I noticed vibrant party lights twinkling at the front and cheerful balloons hovering near the door. The home exuded a festive charm, with party-goers arriving amidst echoes of music and laughter drifting from the backyard.

"Do you want me to pick you up?" Emir asked.

I shook my head with a small smile. "I'm meeting Phuong-Vy and will sleep at her house," I replied, even though I was bending the truth. I was planning to stay over at Ninu's and he would drop me off at Phuong-Vy's place the following morning.

Emir nodded, and with a final wave, he drove off.

I strolled with Lux down the driveway and toward the side gate, my heart fluttering with anticipation. The patio area had been transformed: delicate, twinkling lights hung from the rafters, casting a warm glow over rows of chairs arranged around a DJ station in the corner. As I walked in, the sea of unfamiliar faces only underscored that these were all Ninu's friends and family. This was destined to be our much-anticipated official debut, and the butterflies in my stomach swelled with every step. I gripped Lux's leash a little tighter, finding solace in the gentle presence of the happy dog.

A clear path opened up for us as guests eyed Lux with a blend of curiosity and adoration. Unruffled by the bustling revellers, Lux trotted by my side. I soon spotted Ninu standing with his back turned; a friendly gesture from someone in the crowd prompted him to turn around. His face brightened immediately, a genuine beam of pleasure lighting his features as he took in my appearance. When his eyes fell on Lux, his smile widened even further.

"He's for you," I said softly, handing him the leash.

Ninu's eyes shimmered with emotion as he knelt, gently stroking Lux's head. The dog, ever affectionate, licked Ninu's face, eliciting a warm, radiant smile from him. A woman with striking features reminiscent of Ninu sidled up, her eyes dancing with joy as she looked at Lux.

"He looks just like Brownie," Ninu's mother remarked, her voice filled with wonder. "It's as if he were reincarnated."

I explained, "I've been calling him Lux while trying to find his owner, but of course, you can rename him however you'd like."

"Lux. That's a wonderful name." Ninu leaned in to give Lux a big, affectionate hug, and the dog accepted the embrace with a cheerful spirit. Straightening up, Ninu introduced me, "Mama, this is Seka. My girlfriend."

His mother extended her hand warmly. "I've heard so much about you," she said, her smile inviting and kind.

"Me too," I replied, feeling a rush of warmth at the introduction.

Ninu then called over his father, a man sharing the tall build of his son but with a softer, rounder midsection. "Come meet Seka," he said. I shook his hand. A crowd gathered; Ninu's siblings were introduced in rapid succession, followed by his aunts, uncles, and cousins. The names and faces, a delightful blur of kinship, swirled around me.

"We'll go settle Lux and be right back," Ninu offered gently, wrapping an arm around my shoulders as we drifted away from the lively party area and behind his bungalow. "It's a bit overwhelming."

"You have a big family," I murmured in awe and amusement.

He laughed heartily. "I know. They're like an army. You'll get the hang of who's who before long."

Just beyond the main area, behind the bungalow, lay a little homestead with chickens pecking about, a rabbit hutch, and a dog kennel. "I'll clean this properly tomorrow. But for now, Lux will be just fine out here," Ninu said as he filled a water bowl.

I handed him a shopping bag with the dog food I'd bought. "I already fed him, so you can feed him tomorrow."

Ninu tied Lux with a chain. He stood and hugged me. "This is the best birthday present I've ever had. How did you find him?"

"He was handed in without a microchip. I put up flyers and kept him at my house. As time passed, it was certain we wouldn't be able to find the owner. I've had him for a month now, so we would have found them by now," I delivered my pre-prepared lie.

"I'm so happy," he murmured, his eyes lingering on the twilight sky that stretched endlessly behind us. We stood together on a gentle hill, the stars glittering like scattered diamonds against the inky canvas of night. Slowly, we began to sway in a rhythm as natural as the night breeze.

"How does it feel to be 25?" I asked, my voice soft against the backdrop of the nocturnal hum.

"Pretty fabulous. I feel like my life is finally falling into place," he replied, a warm glow lighting his face. Leaning in, we shared a kiss. "We should head back," he suggested gently.

Taking my hand, we made our way toward the lively party, the raucous sounds growing louder with each step. As we neared, the walls of laughter and conversation grew thicker, the crowd expanding with each new arrival. Amid the welcoming chaos, Ninu and I separated from the throng as the newcomers enveloped him in warm embraces. I lingered at the edge of the gathering, drink in hand, standing slightly apart from the pulsating crowd.

His mother approached and took her place beside me. "So what do you do?"

"I'm studying to be a veterinarian," I answered.

"That's wonderful. You and Ninu seem to have so much in common," she continued, nodding with quiet approval.

I offered a slight nod in return, and she probed a little further. "What about your family?"

"It's just me, my mother, and my brother," I explained.

"And your father isn't here with you?" she pressed, a note of sadness creeping into her voice.

"He went missing in Srebrenica three years ago," I replied, the pain in my voice barely masked.

"Missing?" Concern flickered across her face, the worry lines drawing her brow together.

"During the war. He was trying to escape, but we never learned if he made it. Honestly, we suspect he didn't survive, but his remains have never been found." I swallowed the lump in my throat, loathing this part of the conversation. If I admitted that he had died in the war, it might have brought a morbid finality to the discussion. But the truth was more ambiguous: he was missing until, perhaps one day, his bones and confirmation of death could offer closure.

Just then, his father joined our circle. "Seka was just mentioning that her father is missing," his mother told him gently.

"I'm so sorry to hear that. It's so hard when there isn't a body to bid farewell. My sister's husband lost his father in the Vietnam War—he was a Nasho, and they never recovered him," came the empathetic response.

I knew from Alyssa that Nashos were National Servicemen who were conscripted; their names were selected by lottery, and they had no choice but to enlist—or face imprisonment.

"Wars are terrible business, aren't they? No one wins, only leaving behind sorrow, death, and pain," he observed, taking a slow sip of his beer.

I nodded in silent agreement.

Then, his mother shifted the conversation with another pointed question. "So if you're Bosnian, does that mean you're Muslim?"

"Yes, but I'm not practising," I replied, tilting the beer in my hand with a trace of nonchalance.

She looked at me, confused. "But Muslims don't drink alcohol. Oh," she said with a soft gasp, her features relaxing into a clearer understanding, "So that's why you're not wearing a headscarf."

I explained, "No, Bosnians in general don't wear headscarves. My mother wears one only when she prays."

"So your mother is practising," she inferred.

I nodded.

"But do you go to the mosque?" she asked

"I do go, mostly for family events, although I don't really pray," I admitted softly.

"For Ninu, his Catholic faith is very important. He attends church every weekend. I'm sure it's something he would eventually expect his wife to embrace."

She looked at me expectantly. I stared at the floor. I knew that I would never practice any religion.

His father interjected, "They're not talking marriage yet. It's early days. Let the kids enjoy themselves."

A flicker of annoyance passed over her face before she subdued it. Amidst the lively clamour of the party, I felt a growing desire to escape.

"There you are. Let's dance," Nina said, taking my hand and leading me onto the dance floor.

The music enveloped us as we moved in rhythm, and I closed my eyes, trying to block out his mother's disapproving gaze. Her silent judgement mirrored what my mother would undoubtedly express. If she ever discovered I was dating a Catholic, she would likely disown me, perhaps even insist I leave home, accusing me of bringing shame upon the family. Deep down, I always knew this relationship was destined to be fleeting, yet I had let myself believe, if only for a few precious moments.

As we danced under the dim, flickering lights, tears mingled with the sheen of sweat on my face, creating a salty mixture that trickled down my cheeks. Though I was aware of the inevitable end, I couldn't shake this profound sense of loss that weighed heavily on my heart.

19-Hara Kiri

I came home from work and found the Bosnian newspaper on the table. I usually didn't read it, but it was sitting there, benign and unassuming. I was eating lunch and flicked the page. When I saw Miroslav's face, I quickly stopped.

The food became ash in my mouth. I spat it into a serviette and read, my skin heating up.

War Criminal joins chorus of Genocide Deniers

Former soldier and bus driver Miroslav Vlahović, who was uncovered as a war criminal in our newspaper last week, has been interviewed by the Serb local newspaper, where he states that the genocide is a lie. He made a statement that he was never at Potočari and was not a witness to the 'fictional genocide' the Bosnians have invented.

A source in the Bosnian Embassy has uncovered the following records for Vlahović. In his application for citizenship on humanitarian grounds, he listed that he was a refugee after his home in Medeno Polje was ethnically cleansed by Bosnians.

In his civil life, Miroslav was a bus driver, and in army records obtained from Serbia, he is listed as a soldier, duty transport driver, from June 1992 to September 1994.

Convicted war criminal Janko Bogdanović gave testimony that the Serb bus drivers who were transporting Muslim men and boys to the killing pits were required to shoot a civilian so that they too were implicated in the war.

Miroslav was not just an innocent victim of Serb might, he was complicit in the massacre and now that his role has been revealed, he is attempting to rewrite history.

Anger pulsed through me like a wildfire in my stomach as I crumpled the newspaper, its cheap ink smudging into an indelible stain on my fingers. He had to pay. The coward was trying to erase his shameful past and gloss over the truth.

I recalled the adrenaline rush from confronting Tom, how he'd pleaded for mercy. Now it was Miroslav's turn to feel my wrath.

Standing at the sink, washing dishes under lukewarm water, Mama shuffled in. Her swollen eyelids sagged with exhaustion.

"Did you read it?" I nodded towards the crumpled newspaper on the kitchen table.

She acknowledged silently.

"We'll bring him down eventually. Justice will catch up."

"I don't want to talk about it," Mama said, her voice weary as she switched on the stove for her morning coffee ritual.

"Has Emir found out?" I asked.

She nodded again. "His friends told him."

"Where is he?"

"Who knows?" She shrugged slightly.

We sat together, sipping bitter but comforting coffee, while watching news programs about politics and current events fill the screen with endless chatter. Once she left for work, ready to face another day of routine struggles, I tried to snatch some sleep after last night's episode with Tom playing over in my mind like a broken record.

In bed later that afternoon behind drawn curtains with daylight peeking through cracks—sleep finally took hold—my feverish dreams replayed vivid scenes: Miroslav kneeling helpless at gunpoint reciting confessions he'd rather hide; how I'd squeeze every bit of truth before serving final justice upon him; retribution's chilling promise kept circling within those twisted visions...

When Emir returned home around midnight—the creak of our front door broke into sleep-filled silence—I ventured out and found him at the dining table with cluttered phonebooks scattered across the table before him.

"We're getting close to finding him. I was at my friend's place and we went through the phonebook, calling all the Serb names, trying to track down someone who knows Miroslav Vlahović. I found Slobodan Đokić. He said he'd poke around the community and get back to me," Emir murmured, a spark of determination in his eyes.

"You spoke to Zora's dad?" A chill swept over me, freezing my insides. All this time, I had known exactly where Zora was, yet she remained oblivious about my whereabouts.

"Yeah. I gave him our number for when he has news. But now we should make a list of other Serbs we knew in Yugoslavia."

"How are they?" Curiosity gnawed at me like an insistent itch.

"They're fine," Emir replied nonchalantly, finger tracing under scattered lines in the phonebook until it paused on a name he underlined with heavy intention. "We didn't talk much; just mentioned Babo."

"Oh." My knees nearly buckled beneath me as memories of Zora tumbled into today's reality from their hidden compartment inside my mind. She would have to wait—tomorrow's challenge—but capturing Miroslav before Emir took precedence tonight.

Once Emir was beaten by exhaustion and slinked off to bed, I packed essentials: rope, masking tape, gun, ketamine, white bandages—the tools for ensuring a confession by any means necessary awaited in my backpack.

I slid Ramo's ring onto my finger alongside my silver coin—a souvenir that I would use to reawaken his memory. Looking in the mirror and seeing my dark hair was a relief. My skin looked lighter, my hair darker. I looked like me.

I still had Ninu's battered truck, its old paint faded from countless journeys. I had parked it several blocks away, hidden from view so my mother wouldn't confront me with her probing, uncomfortable questions. At the quiet hour of 1 am, when the world was wrapped in silence, I drove slowly toward Miroslav's house. The curtains were drawn inside, yet a solitary square of light shone from the living room window.

I carefully parked on the street behind his house, directly adjacent to where he slept. The chill of the night air roused every sense as I jumped out of the truck and made my way up the narrow, unlit driveway. A locked fence stood as a barrier between the front and back yards, but my practised agility served me well as I scaled it with ease, the backpack's weight cinched securely to my back.

Moving silently, I approached the back door and slid my key into the lock, turning it with calculated precision. In one smooth motion, I pushed the door open, careful not to disturb the silence. I withdrew the cold metal of a gun from the zippered pocket of my black jacket; its surface catching a glint of activity from the dim corridor. The television's glow in the living room cast long, sinister shadows along the hallway as I gently closed the door. Each step was measured and deliberate, relying on the steady hum of the television to mask any trace of my presence.

Peering cautiously through a barely open doorway, I saw Miroslav slouched in an armchair. He lay drowsily against the headrest, a soft snore escaping him as he slept in his cotton pyjamas and worn singlet. I raised the gun slowly, its weight settling into my hand as I pointed it directly at him. I stepped into the living room where an open can of beer sat innocently on a cluttered coffee table. I retrieved a small vial from my other pocket, uncorking it and carefully pouring its contents into the beer. Just a small amount to make him more pliable.

Taking the remote control from beside the can, I muted the television. I had learned that a man caught between sleep and full awareness is at his most dangerous.

Patiently, I waited as Miroslav's breathing grew shallow. His eyes fluttered and then opened, bleary and disoriented. When they finally met mine, he showed no initial shock; his look was of quiet resignation until alertness fully dawned upon him. Slowly, his gaze inched towards a concealed gun, his eyes widening in a mixture of fear and regret as he stiffened in his armchair.

"Zora, what are you doing here?" he murmured, as he sat upright, every muscle tensed.

"Drink your beer," I commanded, gesturing sharply toward the can with the vial-mixed concoction.

He paused, a flicker of confusion crossing his face as he glanced at the can. Then, hesitantly, he straightened, allowing his legs to plant firmly on the cold floor. With trembling hands, he reached for the beer, taking a cautious sip. The taste did nothing to alert his senses—just as I had expected, the bitter blend of ketamine and alcohol masked itself beneath the flavour.

"What are you doing here?" he repeated, a note of desperation in his tone.

"I thought it was time we had a chat," I replied coolly as I stepped backward and switched on the overhead light. The sudden brightness revealed the decay of his once-loved living space: a dark, stained carpet, dirty dishes piled in corners, and clothes scattered in disarray. Every detail screamed neglect.

"What should I call you, since you're not Zora?" he asked in a low voice.

I felt a jolt of surprise ripple through me. "What makes you say that?"

He leaned back, the dim light catching the hardened lines of his face. "After our little chat in my inebriated state, I was terrified you'd spill my secret. I tracked down Slobodan Đokić and even met his daughter, Zora. That's when I realised I'd been deceived. So why don't you introduce yourself properly?"

I paused, the weight of old memories filling the space between us, and said, "Seka Torlak."

"Should I know you?" he questioned, his voice was wary.

A thin smile played at the corner of my mouth as I reached for something hidden beneath my blouse. "Maybe this will jog your memory." With deliberate calm, I unclasped my necklace and flung it at him. The small, worn coin struck his chest with a pronounced thunk that echoed in the heavy silence.

For a long moment, his face registered nothing but a blank stare. Slowly, almost hesitantly, he picked up the coin. His eyes swept over the faded image of Tito emblazoned on its front, his finger tracing the edges of the weathered photo as if trying to awaken buried recollections.

"You can keep your silver," I spat, my voice seething with disdain. "It's a reminder of your silver town—an echo of your past long after you're gone from here."

He met my glare briefly before his expression shifted. I watched as recognition slowly dawned; his features tightened, a flush of shame spreading across his cheeks, and he averted his eyes.

"You remember now!" I insisted, my voice trembling.

He nodded slowly. "My memories are cloudy that night. We drank until alcohol dulled our reasoning. The army kept us from thinking clearly, so our conscience didn't interrupt their plans."

I recalled the brutal detail, each word a dagger sharpened by pain. "You went out hunting with them, mingling with our own like a wolf prowling for blood."

His tone shifted to one of bitter justification. "I needed money. I was desperate to find gold and jewellery—anything I could sell to start a new life for my wife and family. I believed it was all we were owed after the Bosnians cleansed us from our village. They burned my home, my parents' home—the only life we had known for a hundred years under the Vlahović name. And after the Bosnians came, it was as if our existence was erased from the earth."

I countered fiercely, "That wasn't my fault. I did nothing to force your family from their land."

"And I wasn't responsible for yours," he replied, voice low and despairing. "This is the way of wars—the innocent suffer, while corrupt commanders pull the strings from behind closed doors."

For once, we found mutual ground in that grim admission.

Then I levelled a final accusation, my voice rising with bitter recollection. "Do you remember what happened to me that night? You and your friends wanted to take me with you, to violate me. The only reason that didn't happen was because I began menstruating."

He took a long, shuddering sip from his beer, his eyes welling up with tears. "That wasn't me," he murmured hoarsely. "I had nothing to do with that. I have daughters of my own—children I love. I was only there to get some jewellery or money. But when I saw what they were doing... I left."

I pressed on, anguish mingling with fury. "You left. The girl they took ended her life—her body was later retrieved by UN soldiers. They cut through factory beams to bring her down. Do you really believe that you absolve yourself of guilt by leaving?"

He didn't say a word, his head bowed in defeat.

"You're not innocent, and don't you dare pretend you are," I spat.

His eyes remained downcast as he whispered, "No, I'm not innocent. I know that. There is blood on my hands."

I hurled the crumpled newspaper at him. "And what about your lies? The lies that there was no genocide, you know there was," I snarled.

He let the newspaper drift to the floor. "I had to. I had to protect my family," he murmured.

"You mean you have to protect yourself," I retorted sharply. Slowly, deliberately, I lifted the gun, its cold metal glinting under the harsh light, and aimed it steadily at him. "I'm going to let you have a taste of your own medicine. You're going to feel what it is to be the one terrorised. I want you to die."

He shook his head slowly as if resigned to an inevitable fate. "You think it's that simple. You think you can pull the trigger and just walk away, unchanged. No," he said, his tone mournful as he continued, "When you kill, you kill a part of yourself. You will never be the same person."

"Shut up!" I roared, the sound echoing off the barren walls around us. "Don't you dare lecture me!"

With a heavy sigh of surrender, he raised his hands slowly. "Do what you have to do. But know that this will haunt you for the rest of your life."

"Does he haunt you?" I demanded, tossing him a faded photograph of Ramo. "What about him?" Then I extended another photo, one of my father. "Do you remember them?" I asked, my words trembling with accusation.

He carefully picked up the pictures, scrutinising them as if trying to stitch together memories from fragments of a long-lost past. "I don't remember. I'm sorry," came his soft reply, his fingers gingerly returning the photos to me. "There were so many of them. So many men, so many boys. It is impossible to say."

"Here. Make a confession," I commanded, as I placed a spiral ring notebook and a pen on the table between us. "Write down everything you remember from that day—the names of the people who were with you, who did what, the bus you drove, the locations of the pits. I want landmarks noted so they can be found. I want it all written down in detail."

He hesitated. "And then what?"

"And then you die. Everyone will think it's suicide, and your confession will be printed. Your life, your sins, will finally have some meaning," I explained coldly.

As he scribbled in the notebook, his hand trembling with the burden of confession, I watched silently.

Finally, I slid a folded envelope with a sticky note across the table. On it, the name Alyssa Jones was scrawled in careful handwriting. "Write down this name and address on the envelope," I instructed. "I'm sending this letter to Alyssa. Once I've finished with you, she will receive it and use the information to publish your confession. The UN will have enough details to start a real investigation. They will uncover the graves of those missing. And they will finally give those souls the burial they deserve."

A moment of reluctant understanding passed as he nodded slowly. "You're right. This is the best way. This way, I can give justice to those who need it, and I won't bring further harm to my family."

He finished writing and sealed the envelope with a slow, deliberate twist of his wrist. I slipped the letter into my pocket. "Now it's time for you to die," I said.

He sank to his knees, and I pressed the cold metal of the gun against his temple, staging the scene as a tragic suicide. I imagined that a clean shot—just through the temple—would keep the police at bay. The gun, left behind with his fingerprints, would be the perfect prop, and the letter, destined for Alyssa, was to serve as a neatly wrapped suicide note.

"It's not that easy," he murmured. "I hesitated too when I had to kill the man. I didn't want to do it."

"Shut up." I growled. "I'm going to kill you." I inhaled deeply, mentally preparing to pull the trigger, yet my finger hesitated, caught between duty and doubt.

Ramo materialised from a shadowed corner, his form stretching toward me like a protective spectre. "Seka, no. Don't do it," he pleaded, his voice filled with an earnest urgency that echoed through the dim room.

"Shut up. Shut up. He deserves it." My voice wavered as my trembling finger hovered over the trigger.

My hand went slack, and Miroslav delivered a swift kick to my feet. I tumbled, colliding with the table before rolling onto the cold, unforgiving floor. Rising steadily, Miroslav took the gun from my limp grasp.

A shudder of apprehension ran through me as he stepped forward. The flickering light carved menacing shadows across his face, transforming him into the spectre of that grim night at the factory, when death had seemed an inescapable fate. I flinched and closed my eyes, turning my head away from the dark vision that now stood before me.

"Stop it," he roared. "I'm not going to hurt you." His large, calloused hand reached out roughly and lifted me from the floor, guiding me onto a worn-out sofa. "I was lost for so long, paralysed by uncertainty," he intoned, his eyes never leaving mine. "But now I see the path forward. Take your things and leave."

I gathered my backpack with trembling hands and edged toward the door, lagging with hesitant steps, half-expecting him to block my exit.

"Are you really going to let me walk out of here?" I asked.

"Yes," he answered.

"Even with the letter?" I pressed, the envelope still burning in my pocket.

"Yes." He turned away, dismissing me. "Post it. It won't matter after tonight."

I stepped into the hallway, a brief flutter of relief filling me. He should die.

I opened the front door, but I froze mid-step. Heart pounding, I closed the door again, and turned. The gun was now pressed to his mouth, his eyelids gently closing as if succumbing to a resigned fate. All I had to do was turn away, but my feet wouldn't move. Ramo was still in the shadows, watching me, guiding me back to myself.

"No, don't," I shouted, the plea rising desperately from within.

Slowly, he opened his eyes.

I remembered the loving way he spoke about his daughters. The guilt was written on his face as he spoke about the massacre and his part in it. Was another death the solution to this madness? "Please, put the gun down. You don't need to do this," I implored. I pulled the letter from my pocket and tore it apart. "It's gone. The letter is gone. There is no reason for you to kill yourself."

He slowly removed the cold, metallic barrel of the gun from his mouth. "Why did you do that?" After everything you did to try to get that confession."

"There's been enough killing," I replied softly. "I don't want to be like that."

He nodded, a silent understanding passing between us. Carefully, he opened the gun, the metallic click echoing in the quiet room, then took out the bullets, placing them gently in a drawer. Handing the now harmless gun back to me, he said, "Call your journalist. I'll give the interview." He turned and made his way to the kitchen. "Are you hungry? I'll make us breakfast."

The first light of dawn was creeping over the horizon, painting the sky with hues of pink and orange. We had spent countless hours locked in a tense confrontation, and now a new day was beginning.

Picking up the phone, I dialled Alyssa's number. Her voice crackled on the line, and she assured me she would arrive by 10 am.

I sat down to the breakfast Miroslav prepared, the aroma of freshly cooked food filling the air. After eating, I busied myself tidying the house, the rhythmic movements providing a sense of calm. Meanwhile, Miroslav showered, the sound of water running a soothing backdrop, and emerged dressed in neat pants and a crisp shirt, ready to face what lay ahead.

20-Interview

When Alyssa arrived, I sat on the faded couch in the living room, watching as Miroslav met her at the front door with a tense nod. The late afternoon light cast long shadows across the room.

"I was surprised to receive your phone call, Miroslav," Alyssa said as she crossed the threshold. When her eyes landed on me; she paused in the doorway, uncertainty etched across her face, hesitant to expose my true identity.

"He knows I'm Seka," I replied quietly, rising from the couch and motioning for her to sit.

"I'm here to tell the truth," Miroslav announced with a firm gesture toward the chair opposite him. Alyssa produced her tape recorder and notepad.

I drifted into the adjoining kitchen, leaning against the cool, tiled countertop while I listened. Miroslav detailed satellite images and meticulously drawn maps pinpointing each mass grave site. His words painted a morbid picture: the approximate numbers, the haunting descriptions of the victims.

Out in the backyard, I stared through the window. My thoughts spiralled to Ramo—wondering if he was lost in one of those pits, one of the men whose fate Miroslav had sealed with his own hands. For years, a torrent of hatred had burned inside me, a raw rage that craved vengeance. Now I was enveloped in a perplexing numbness, caught between retribution and relief.

"You are aware that you will be indicted on murder charges?" Alyssa said.

Miroslav nodded, his eyes heavy with resignation. "Maybe I will atone for what I did. If more people are found, it might help."

"I will need to contact the War Tribunal—have you arranged to be indicted and secured a new identity so that you can testify?"

Miroslav offered another quiet nod in response.

Alyssa concluded the interview by turning off her recorder. "I'll publish this after you've been given a safe identity." She stepped toward the door.

Miroslav and I shared a long, solemn look—two combatants entangled in a deadly struggle for so long that now, in the silence of resignation, nothing more needed to be said.

"Take care, Seka," he murmured, nodding as he closed the door behind me.

Stepping outside, I followed Alyssa into the cool morning air. The relief was almost palpable, as if the heavy walls of that house had been keeping not just secrets, but the weight of my past. With each step, it felt like I was leaving behind a long, harrowing chapter. I had accomplished my mission: I had uncovered a war criminal. Now, the slow but inevitable march toward justice would begin in earnest.

"How did you get him to talk?" Alyssa asked.

Adjusting the strap of my worn backpack and aware of the cold metal of the hidden gun inside, I replied almost nonchalantly, "I convinced him that his conscience was a burden he should finally shed."

Her eyes flickered with disbelief, yet she let the moment pass without further probing. "You did it," Alyssa said softly. "What will you do now?"

I shrugged, feeling the odd displacement of emotions—a sense of detachment and the surreal notion that everything in my life had become strangely distant.

"If you ever decide to switch careers and become a journalist, I'd be happy to help you make that change. You have the makings of an exceptional investigative reporter," she offered.

We exchanged a firm handshake, and I climbed into Ninu's battered old truck, its engine humming as I set off. I steered toward Brimbank Park, where the winding path beckoned through clusters of whispering trees, leading me down to the flowing Maribyrnong River. The water glistened under the gentle caress of the morning light as I strolled along its edge, until I reached the river's deepest, most secluded section. A lone jogger passed in the distance, a fleeting silhouette.

I unzipped my backpack and sifted through its contents until I clutched the cold metal of the gun. I arched my arm back and hurled it away. It sailed through the still air and splashed into the dark river with a muted plop. I felt relief as the weapon sank beneath the rippling surface. I recalled the old saying—that it's not the gun but the hand that wields it that brings harm. I remembered vividly how the weapon had shifted me, the power I'd felt over Tom and later Miroslav. Although it was people who must ultimately pull the trigger, the mere presence of the gun had the uncanny power to taint a person's mind.

When I got Mama bustling around inside, tidying up with an air of determined calm. She told me Emir was out with his friends. I quickly called a few of his contacts until I finally found him, and told him he had to return home immediately.

The front door crashed and Emir demanded. "What's going on?"

Mama, caught in mid-clean with the vacuum still humming, looked up in surprise.

"I need to speak with you both," I said, holding my voice steady. I waited until Mama powered off the vacuum, as I gestured for Emir to sit on the worn couch.

"I found Miroslav," I began.

Emir's eyes flickered with a fiery satisfaction as he leaned forward. "Give me his address. I'm going to make him pay," he snarled.

"There's no need," I replied calmly. "He's already been interrogated by Alyssa, and he spilled every detail about the massacre. She's passing the information onto the Crimes Tribunal. He's going to be arrested soon."

"And then he'll be locked away in some comfortable cell at The Hague for years. That's bullshit," Emir fumed, pacing back and forth across the room, as he clenched and unclenched his fists. "He needs to pay."

I sank into my chair and spoke in a low, measured tone. "I felt the same way, Emir. That's why I broke into his house with a gun in hand. I held it to his temple, filled with the urge to end it all."

Mama gasped, her hand flying to her mouth. "You didn't..." she whispered.

"I nearly did," I admitted. "I almost pulled the trigger." I shied away from telling them that Ramo came to save me. He was my secret.

Emir's knees buckled, and he sank onto the couch as if drained of all his strength.

"And if I had..." I continued, my tone turning sombre, "I would be in jail right now. Would that be fair to you, to me, or Mama?"

Tears welled in Mama's eyes as she began to sob softly, her voice quivering. "I could have lost you, too. I could have lost you both," she cried.

I reached out, taking her hand. "But you didn't lose me. I pulled myself back from that edge, and I'm telling you all of this because I came so close to crossing that line. Close to becoming a killer and ruining all of our lives forever. If you do anything rash, Emir—if you go to see him or hurt him—you'll only be inviting more pain upon me and Mama."

Emir nodded slowly, his eyes downcast.

"Where's the gun?" Mama's voice trembled with worry.

"I threw it into a river."

"Do you promise? Swear on your father's grave!" she demanded, her eyes blazing with desperation.

"I swear on my father's grave that I threw the gun away. No one will ever find it to use it," I promised.

The shrill tone of the telephone shattered the fragile stillness. Emir rose and answered the call. As soon as the caller's voice was identified, his entire demeanour transformed—the muscles in his body tightened as if bracing against an incoming storm. "Slobodan, hello," he said in a cool tone.

It was Zora's father on the other end of the line.

"Thank you for calling back. I don't require that information anymore." A pause followed, hanging heavily in the air as Slobodan replied. "Mama's fine." Emir's gaze shifted to our mother, silently asking if she wanted to talk. With a quiet shake of her head, she rose from her seat and left the living room. "I'm sorry, Seka just told me she's not around," he continued after another thoughtful pause. "Zora wants to speak to Seka." His eyes met mine across the room.

Time itself seemed to hesitate. I had dodged this confrontation for so long. Tentatively, I reached out for the phone.

"She's right here," Emir announced calmly, passing the handset into my hesitant grasp.

"Hello, Seka," Slobodan's voice resonated through the receiver, his tone heavy with regret. "I was so sorry to hear about your father." There was a distinct quaver, a raw, teary note in his voice as he continued, "He was my best friend for nearly twenty years."

"I know. He loved you too," I replied softly.

"Anyway, here's Zora for you."

Another pause ensued, as the phone was handed over to Zora.

"Seka," came her voice at last—a sound I had not heard in seven long years. Although her tone had deepened slightly compared to our voices when we were fifteen, the cadence and familiar inflection lingered, her sentences rising ever so gently at the close.

"Hello," I greeted her, gripping the handset like a lifeline. Emir quietly slipped away from the living room.

"I'm so sorry about your father," Zora said, her voice imbued with sorrow.

"Thank you. And what about you? Is everyone okay?" I inquired.

"Yes, we all made it to Australia in 1993. We spent some time in a refugee camp in Serbia before coming over," she explained.

"So did we. But we didn't arrive until 1996," I noted, feeling the weight of lost time slip through our shared histories.

"We've both been living here now for the past three years. We lost so much time waiting, wondering, reaching out. I even checked the phone book now and then, but I never saw your name," she added.

"Oh, I think we have a silent number," I replied. It was a family decision to pay extra so our phone number would remain private. Mama had always been vigilant about keeping our identity hidden, aware that Slobodan and his family, along with several Serb friends, were here in Australia. She had never wanted them to intrude on our carefully guarded world.

A moment of silence passed as she processed this revelation. "Do you want to meet?" she asked.

That spark of courage and candour was characteristic of her. I wasn't entirely sure if meeting face-to-face was a wise idea, yet the pull was irresistible. Now that our voices had bridged years of separation, a deep yearning to understand every detail surged within me.

"Okay," I agreed, and we arranged to meet at Degraves Lane in the city's heart—a narrow lane facing the bustling Flinders Street Station.

I placed the phone back on its cradle, and Mama and Emir quietly drifted into the room.

"I'm going to meet Zora," I announced, hoping for a spark of understanding in their eyes.

"Is that a good idea?" Mama questioned, her brow furrowing with concern.

"I want to see her. I need to hear what's happening with her," I replied.

"That's your decision," Mama reached for the vacuum cleaner. "Just make sure you tell her I don't want to meet with any of them."

"Nor I," Emir echoed.

Mama switched on the vacuum cleaner, its roar filling the room and signalling the end of our conversation. I turned away and headed to my bedroom.

As we'd agreed, I waited in the cosy, dimly lit cafe, the murmur of conversation and clinking cups around me heightened my anticipation. My eyes swept over the room, meticulously scanning every face, desperately seeking hers amid a procession of blonde heads fluttering like painted figures on a busy canvas. And then I saw her—Zora, making her way toward me.

She reached my table, and as I rose to greet her, we stood awkwardly facing one another. In that suspended moment, we exchanged tentative glances, each of us hesitating about how to bridge the chasm of lost time: a kiss, a hug, a simple handshake? We hadn't seen each other in seven long years—a lifetime that had transformed the girl I once knew into an enigmatic adult. I struggled to reconcile the vibrant, carefree child of memory with the composed woman standing before me. For years, I had followed her like a silent shadow, never daring to see her face up close.

Breaking the stillness, I extended my hand. Though every fibre of me yearned to pull her into an enveloping embrace, I was gripped by an inexplicable fear of closeness—a need to guard both of us by keeping an invisible barrier in place. A brief flash of disappointment darkened her eyes before she hesitantly accepted my hand.

We sat down, the space between us charged with unspoken regrets and memories.

"I wish I'd known you were here sooner," she whispered, her voice soft and laced with a hint of longing, "so we could truly talk."

"Me too," I replied, my words tumbling in a clumsy lie. How could I reveal that I had known where she was all along, that I had chosen to keep my distance rather than face the overwhelming torrent of emotions that seeing her would unleash? Trying to steer the conversation away from the unspoken, I asked, "How are you doing? Are you studying?"

Zora nodded slowly, her eyes lighting up with a gentle enthusiasm. "I'm studying to become a teacher. I'm finishing my final rounds, and then I'll be looking for a job next year."

"A teacher? I always remembered you talking about wanting to be a veterinarian," I remarked, my voice edged with surprise.

Her smile was wistful. "Dreams change, you know? I've realised that teaching is truly my calling. And what about you?"

"I'm in my first year of my degree to be a veterinarian," I shared.

"That's wonderful," she said warmly

She had moved on, embraced a world of possibility I had once longed for.

Zora's tone softened into a curious inquiry. "Do you have a boyfriend?"

I nodded. "It's new. I'm not even sure whether it's going to be something serious. What about you?"

Happiness danced in her eyes as she revealed, "I'm engaged. We're hoping to marry next year, once I begin working. Novak is a plumber."

"He's Serb?" I asked.

She nodded. "Yes, our families came to Australia around the same time; they were friends. There was some playful flirting between us, but it never felt real until year 12."

Her words struck me like a dagger—here she was, poised to marry her childhood sweetheart, while I was haunted by the loss of the love I once cherished. It felt as though her life had flowed onward, untouched by the heartache that had left me feeling shattered.

"But what about your boyfriend?" she asked.

"He doesn't matter," I replied with quiet resignation. "We're not meant to last anyway. Our families would never accept it. He's not Bosnian."

"That doesn't matter," she insisted gently. "As long as you love each other, nothing else should stand in your way."

My voice rose, trembling with a mix of anger and despair. "If it doesn't matter, why are you marrying a Serb?"

Her eyes widened in surprise and hurt as she studied my face, "Did I say something wrong? You seem upset."

"You didn't say anything wrong," I began softly. "You were just telling me about your perfect life—the picture-perfect family you still have, the love of your life by your side, the promising career stretching out before you. There's no loss in your past."

"Yes, I did," she said, her voice heavy with regret. "I lost my grandparents. My uncles were killed in the village when the Muslims attacked. And our home was taken from us."

A bitter laugh escaped her lips. "Well, I lost everything else." I paused, the silence thick with memories and unspoken pain. "I knew where you were," I confessed. "I always knew. Since the moment I arrived in Tuzla, I clung to your address as if it were a lifeline. Alyssa, a journalist I met in Srebrenica, gave it to me. I found myself coming by regularly, seeking glimpses of you. I followed you to the church, hiding in the shadows, listening as you sat there while the priest derided Srebrenica as a fabrication, proclaiming that the massacre was a myth. And your entire family sat, listening to those poisonous lies."

"We never believed it," she interjected softly. "We knew there was some truth to it."

"But you chose to sit there anyway," I countered. "I always knew this would be a mistake. The girls we once were are forever lost to time. This is the bitter reality now. I have nothing left to give you but bitterness. I understand, deep down, that it isn't your fault. You never deliberately caused harm, yet I find myself unable to let go, or forgive. I wish that I had never come."

"Please, Seka," she pleaded softly. "We just need to talk, to rediscover each other as we once did."

Why couldn't I forgive her? Why couldn't I accept her friendship? There was a bitterness inside me. Something that couldn't rest. To take Zora back into my life was to accept the person I was before the war. I had to keep the two separate: the Seka I was before the war died on 11 July 1995. She believed that Serbs and Muslims could be friends. That nationality didn't matter. What mattered was the person. The Seka I was now couldn't. After seeing so much death and carnage, suffering so much and so bitterly, I had changed. I was darker, more suspicious of people, unable to accept them at face value. In that moment, the unbridgeable gulf between past and present lay bare.

Although I was certain that Zora wasn't evil, a cloud of uncertainty lingered over what she and her family might have done upon returning to Serbia. Questions haunted me: did her father and brothers enlist in the Serb army? Were they involved in the killing of Muslims? A knot of hypocrisy twisted in my stomach, as I knew my brother was a soldier who had taken the lives of Serbs as well, and therein lay the heart of the problem.

"I'm sorry. I think it's best if we don't see each other again." I stood, hesitating for a moment, searching for the right words. "I truly hope life is kind to you."

With a heavy heart, I rose from my seat and walked away.

21-Scribe

Ninu hefted the well-worn couch out to the dusty ute. Meanwhile, Phuong-Vy and I carefully boxed up each piece of her once lively kitchen.

"Are you sure about this?" I asked softly.

She offered a slight, resolute nod. "It's time I moved in with my sister. After Tom, I don't feel safe by myself anymore."

"But she's going to expect you to take care of her kids and keep the house spotless," I countered, raising an eyebrow.

She shrugged. "It's a small price to pay for having safety and security," she said, as if she were quoting a well-worn mantra.

"And what about when she begins with the matchmaking?" I pressed.

For a moment, the tension in the room deepened as she said nothing, the silence punctuating the weight of her internal struggle.

"You're not going to go along with it, are you?" I asked after a contemplative pause.

She nodded decisively. "I want to be a part of my community. I've had enough of being an outlier. Nothing good comes from it."

"What do you mean? You have freedom," I pressed.

"To what end? I'll have no one around me when I'm in trouble," she replied quietly, handing me a small box. "These are for you?"

I opened the box to find her contact lenses inside.

"I won't need them anymore," she murmured,.

"So you're giving up? You're going to conform?"

"It's time to grow up," she affirmed, the finality in her voice echoing in the packed room.

Ninu reappeared, effortlessly lifting the heavy dining table over his head. His rippling biceps shimmered with sweat beneath his white t-shirt.

"What will you do about him?" she asked softly once Ninu had stowed the table away in the ute.

"What do you mean?" I retorted, idly labelling a box of plates.

"If your mother and brother find out, they'll disown you. You won't have a family anymore. Do you really think that your relationship with Ninu is built on a solid foundation?" she challenged.

"I don't want to think about this," I admitted. "We're having fun now, and that's all I care about."

"Okay. But you're going to have to decide at some point."

I knew deep down she was right. My relationship with Ninu was a precarious secret that would shatter my entire world if exposed. I had to choose between the conformity that Phuong-Vy embraced, or the unpredictable freedom that beckoned me.

"Okay, I'll change the subject. I read your article."

I'd penned an article for The Argus about how I caught a notorious war criminal, detailing my investigation into

Miroslav. Of course, the version that went public had been carefully edited. The final piece focused on my collaboration with Alyssa, leaving out the dangerous adventures.

"It was amazing," she said, her eyes brightening with pride.

A smile tugged at my lips. "Thank you," I replied, feeling a brief surge of pride.

"And when are you beginning your cadetship?" she inquired.

As soon as I submitted my article, Alyssa arranged an interview with the editor. They offered cadetships at the newspaper—a three-year journey during which I would work as a junior reporter and complete my qualifications to become a full-fledged journalist. The prospect shimmered with promise and the thrill of chasing truth.

I had braced myself for Mama and Emir's disappointment over my career change, but to my surprise, they were incredibly supportive. My stint as an undercover investigator while portraying Zora had won them over. I had been aware for some time that becoming a vet wasn't my dream, but I was too frightened to acknowledge it. Admitting it would have meant embarking on a new path, and I wasn't ready for that leap.

"I start in a month," I said, pressing down the flaps of a cardboard box and sealing it with a strip of tape. "I'm transferring, and luckily, some of my university credits will count toward my journalism degree. Until then, I'll spend the summer working at the vet clinic before starting my new job."

"Your whole life has transformed. How do you feel?"

"Excited," I replied, feeling a thrill of anticipation ripple through me. "For the first time in a long time, I'm excited about my future."

As I spoke, Ninu arrived. He took the box from my hands, and as he leaned down, our lips met in a tender kiss. I felt a comforting reassurance in his presence, grateful to have him as a steadfast part of my future.

A month later, I found myself at the bustling airport, standing on the edge of the runway. The air was filled with the roar of engines and the scent of aviation fuel. Lux watched the aeroplanes taxi by, his ears twitching at every sound, his gaze flickering with curiosity and alertness.

As I surveyed the scene, Miroslav emerged in the distance, flanked by two imposing security guards. He was being escorted to The Hague for his trial under the vigilant watch of Interpol. His strides were steady, yet there was an air of resignation about him.

Miroslav's eyes fell upon Lux, and his pace faltered. When Lux recognised his former owner, he bounded forward with unrestrained joy. Miroslav knelt, his hands reaching to embrace the dog, and Lux leaned into his touch with a gentle whimper.

I approached them slowly, allowing them the moment they both seemed to need. The wind tousled my hair as I observed their reunion in silence.

"I thought he was dead," Miroslav murmured, his voice a mixture of surprise and relief.

I remained silent, giving him the space to process the truth.

"You took him to hurt me," he said, his eyes meeting mine with a mix of accusation and understanding.

I nodded, acknowledging his words.

"Does he have a good owner?" he inquired, his hands cradling Lux's head tenderly, stroking him under the neck where the fur was softest.

"Yes. He is loved. He has plenty of space on the farm to run and be free," I assured him.

"Thank you for bringing him to me," Miroslav said, extending his hand. I took it, feeling the weight of unspoken words in the gesture.

"Are your family coming with you?" I asked, curious about his future.

He gazed into the distance, a shadow passing over his face. "No. They have their lives in Queensland. My wife wants them to have stability. Maybe one day I'll see them again." He lowered his head, pressing his forehead against Lux's, whispering, "Live a good life, my beautiful boy."

With that, he rose, turning towards the boarding gate without another glance back. His silhouette grew smaller as he walked away, consumed by the throng of travellers.

I returned to Ninu's truck, where Lux sat waiting in the passenger seat. As we pulled out of the car park, an aeroplane roared overhead, ascending into the sky.

"Let's take you home, Lux," I said, as we drove away from the chaos of the airport and back towards the haven of Ninu's farm. As the city landscape faded into the rearview mirror, Lux whined softly, a sound of contentment.

BONUS CONTENT

ZORA'S STORY
ESSAY ABOUT WAR CRIMINALS IN AUSTRALIA

https://www.amrapajalic.com/seka-torlak-series.html

Seka Torlak Series

Forged on the war-torn streets of Srebrenica, Seka Torlak fights for justice, retribution and truth.

0.5: The Tree That Stood Still

Srebrenica 1992

In a town shattered by prejudice, two girls forge a friendship that defies the ravages of war...

Seka and Zora have been inseparable, growing up as neighbours and best friends in the once peaceful town of Srebrenica. But as Yugoslavia begins to splinter and nationalism sweeps through the region, their town is torn apart by prejudice and violence. Suddenly, Seka and Zora find themselves on opposite sides of a brutal conflict, their friendship strained by the rising tide of hatred.

As the horrors of war descend upon Srebrenica, Seka and Zora's bond is tested like never before. With nationalist propaganda fuelling distrust andf ear, the streets they once played in become battlegrounds. Amidst the chaos, they must navigate a world where friends can become enemies overnight. Will their friendship endure the storm of war and prejudice, or will it be shattered by the forces tearing their town apart?

Book 1: Time Kneels Between Mountains

Srebrenica, 1992

In a town where survival is a daily battle, there are those who seek justice...

Overnight, Seka Torlak's life as a regular teenager is upended as Srebrenica, her once peaceful town, falls under siege and she faces starvation, shelling, and sniper attacks. When desperately needed antibiotics and food disappear and are sold on the black market, Seka vows to investigate the corruption and bring the culprits to justice.

As the war ravages Srebrenica, Seka's resilience is tested as she navigates loss, fear, and the harsh realities of war. Yet, amidst the devastation, she finds a glimmer of hope as her relationship with Ramo blossoms from friendship to love. But as she fights for justice and love, will Seka triumph, or will the brutal war tear everything she holds dear apart?

Bonus Short Story: Belma's Liberation

In a village shadowed by abuse, there are those with courage who fight for liberation...

Sign up to my newsletter and read *Belma's Liberation* to find out how Seka saved her friend from her abusive father

Book 2: Ghosts Among the Gumtrees

Melbourne, 1997

In a city where the guilty roam free, there are those who seek retribution...

After surviving the brutal siege of Srebrenica, Seka Torlak is trying to rebuild her life as a refugee in Melbourne, 1997. But her fragile peace is shattered when she spots a war criminal responsible for her father's death walking freely in the city. Determined to uncover his true identity and bring him to justice, Seka delves into an investigation that reveals a sinister underbelly of suburbia, where genocide deniers hide in plain sight.

Haunted by memories of war and loss, Seka grapples with the raging conflict within her: the pursuit of justice versus the thirst for retribution. As she navigates this perilous path, she must decide what she is willing to sacrifice for the truth. Will Seka find her salvation, or will she lose her soul in the process?

Bonus Short Story: Zora's Story

In the ruins of war, there are those who cling to memories of friendship...

Sign up to my newsletter and read *Zora's Story* to find out her story in escaping the war

Book 3: Mad Dawn Winter

Riverwood, 1998

In a town submerged with secrets and corruption, there are those who seek the truth...

Seka Torlak, now a journalism cadet, relocates to the tranquil town of Riverwood in 1998, seeking a fresh start. However, her peace is short-lived when she stumbles upon a cold case involving the murder of a formerVietnam Vet. Driven by a grieving mother's plea for justice, Seka begins to uncover a web of secrets that this seemingly idyllic town has buried deep.

In her quest for truth, Seka befriends Dawn Winter, a fellow Bosnian woman haunted by the loss of a friend and ostracized by the townspeople for her tributes to the fallen. As Seka digs deeper, she finds herself entangled in a dangerous game of deceit and loyalty, facing ghosts of the past and present. Will she unravel the truth and deliver justice before it's too late, or will the town's dark secrets consume her?

Bonus Short Story: Art's War

In a time of loss and grief, there are those who pursue the truth...

Sign up to my newsletter and read *Art's Fall* to find out about his investigation first-hand

Bonus Short Story: The Regrets of Ben Hayes

In a war where fear reigns, love remains unspoken...

Sign up to my newsletter and read *The Regrets of Ben Hayes* to find out about his first love during his service as a National Serviceman.

About the author

Amra Pajalic is an award-winning Australian author, educator, and indie publisher known for crafting compelling stories that blend heart, humour, and heritage. Her work explores themes of identity, belonging, and resilience, often drawing from her Bosnian background.

She won the 2009 Melbourne Prize for Literature's Civic Choice Award for her debut novel *The Good Daughter*, re-released as *Sabiha's Dilemma* (PishukinPress, 2022). The anthology she co-edited, *Growing up Muslim in Australia* (Allen and Unwin, 2014), was shortlisted for the 2015 Children's Book Council of the year awards and her memoir *Things Nobody Knows But Me* (Transit Lounge, 2019) was shortlisted for the 2020 National Biography Award. Her short story collection *The Cuckoo's Song* (Pishukin Press) features previously published and prize-winning stories.

Amra is the author of the Sassy Saints series, a young adult contemporary trilogy set in Melbourne's western suburbs. These stories feature smart-mouthed teens, love triangles, fake friends, and fierce girl power, offering a refreshing take on multicultural Australian life.

She is also the creator of the gripping Seka Torlak crime mystery series. Forged on the war-torn streets of Srebrenica, Seka Torlak fights for justice, retribution and truth.

Amra is committed to accessibility and inclusion in publishing. Through her micro-press, PishukinPress, she releases her titles in a wide range of formats—including audiobook, large print, dyslexic font, paperback, ebook, and hardback—to ensure all readers can experience her stories.

When she's not writing, Amra is podcasting on *Amra's Armchair Anecdotes*, mentoring emerging writers, and delivering workshops across Australia on self-publishing, writing craft, and creative resilience.

Amra Pajalić publishes her dark fiction using pen name A. P. Pajalic. She also publishes romance novels under pen name Mae Archer.

goodreads.com/author/show/3310015.Amra_Pajalic

facebook.com/AmraPajalicAuthor/

instagram.com/amrapajalicauthor/

https://twitter.com/AmraPajalic

tiktok.com/@amrapajalic

youtube.com/c/AmraPajalicAuthor

SIGN UP FOR AMRA'S AUTHOR NEWSLETTER

For news, giveaways, bonus material, and sneak peeks, please sign up to her newsletter below.

www.amrapajalic.com

Help Bring the *Seka Torlak* Series to Life—Your Reviews Matter!

Dear Reader,

Thank you for reading *Ghosts Among the Gumtrees*, the second novel in the Seka Torlak series — a story of justice, survival, and resilience set against the scars of war. This series is a labour of love, shaped by years of research and a deep desire to illuminate the histories too often left untold.

Now, I'd love your help. Reviews are the heartbeat of independent publishing — they help readers discover new stories, amplify unheard voices, and keep authors like me creating. Whether you've just finished *Ghosts Among the Gumtrees* or also read *Time Kneels Between Mountains*, your thoughts matter.

A few sentences about what moved you — Seka's courage, the historical depth, or the emotional weight of the story —

can make a world of difference. You can leave a rating or review wherever you bought the book.

Thank you for championing this series and being part of its journey into the world.

Hvala lijepo/Much thanks,

Amra Pajalić

Also by

Seka Torlak Series
The Tree That Stood Still
Time Kneels Between Mountains
Ghosts Among the Gumtrees
Mad Dawn Winter

Memoir
Things Nobody Knows But Me
Growing up Muslim in Australia

Sassy Saints Series
Sabiha's Dilemma
Alma's Loyalty
Jesse's Triumph

Young Adult
The Cuckoo's Song
The Climb

Romance as Mae Archer
Return to Me
Hollywood Dreams

Vintage Dreams

Dark Fiction/Horror as A.P. Pajalic
Woman on the Edge